ALSO BY GLENN BECK

Fiction

The Christmas Sweater

The Christmas Sweater: A Picture Book

The Overton Window

Nonfiction

*Arguing With Idiots: How to Stop Small Minds
and Big Government*

*Glenn Beck's Common Sense: The Case Against
an Out-of-Control Government, Inspired by Thomas Paine*

*An Inconvenient Book: Real Solutions to
the World's Biggest Problems*

The Real America: Messages from the Heart and Heartland

The 7: Seven Wonders That Will Change Your Life

*The Original Argument: The Federalists' Case for the Constitution,
Adapted for the 21st Century*

THE
SNOW ANGEL

GLENN BECK

with Nicole Baart

THRESHOLD EDITIONS **MERCURY RADIO ARTS**

New York   London   Toronto   Sydney   New Delhi

THRESHOLD EDITIONS • MERCURY RADIO ARTS
A Division of Simon & Schuster, Inc.
1230 Avenue of the Americas
New York, NY 10020

First Threshold Editions/Mercury Radio Arts
hardcover edition October 2011

THRESHOLD EDITIONS and colophon are trademarks of
Simon & Schuster, Inc.

For information about special discounts for bulk purchases,
please contact Simon & Schuster Special Sales at 1-866-506-1949
or business@simonandschuster.com.

The Simon & Schuster Speakers Bureau can bring authors to
your live event. For more information or to book an event,
contact the Simon & Schuster Speakers Bureau at 1-866-248-3049
or visit our website at www.simonspeakers.com.

Designed by Ruth Lee-Mui

Manufactured in the United States of America

1   3   5   7   9   10   8   6   4   2

ISBN 978-1-4391-8720-3
ISBN 978-1-4516-4959-8 (ebook)

DEDICATION

This is a story that I have wanted to tell for years. It is my hope that it will wake those up who've been trained to believe in lies like "it's my fault," "it's not so bad," "he won't do it again," or "verbal abuse isn't really abuse." Never forget who you are: a daughter of a Heavenly Father. You have royal heritage, and anyone who makes you feel like less than that is not a man, husband, father, or friend, simply someone who is afraid of you because he knows who you are, but doesn't know who he is.

This book is also dedicated to my sisters, who inspire me, to my mother, who lost her way, and to my wife and daughters, who give me hope. It is also a gift to all the fathers and protectors who try hard every day to be better men than they were yesterday.

THE
SNOW ANGEL

MITCH

December 24, 6:45 A.M.

In the stillness before he opens his eyes, Mitchell Clark is strong. He is young and healthy and brimming with life. His arms are roped muscle, hands calloused from pounding nails and lifting beams. His body is a machine, lithe and powerful.

Mitch stretches a little, and as his feet arch toward the end of the bed, he can feel the ache of a long day in the shallow curve of his lower back. He doesn't mind. The stiffness means that he's worked hard. That he's sweated, spent himself, provided. There is a certain pride in that, a sense of accomplishment that fills him with purpose. I know who I am, Mitch thinks, savoring the hush of dawn, the sound of his own heartbeat in his ears. I am . . . I am . . . but try as he might, he can't finish the thought. It slips away from him and evaporates entirely at the sound of her voice.

"Good morning, Mr. Clark."

Mitch's eyes snap open and take in the square-cut lines of her pink scrubs and the dark ponytail that curves over her slender shoulder. Beneath the title Nurse's Aide, her name tag holds three sparse letters, Kim or Sue or Dee, but he doesn't pay them any attention. His heart is pounding a furious rhythm, and he feels the peace of only a moment before sliding from his grasp.

"Let's get you up, shall we?" She says it kindly, gently, even as she wraps her arms around him to ease him up from the confines of an impossibly narrow bed. She's too small to be lifting him, but all at once he's sitting, and the body he marveled at only a heartbeat before has betrayed him. He hurts. Everywhere.

The twinge in his back is sharp, and his knees throb. His hip, too, but the pain feels familiar. Mitch settles into it even as his hands bunch the sheets beneath him. They're white, and stamped in black at the very edge: The Heritage Home. He's read the words before somewhere, they should mean something to him, but all he can think about is the way his knees poke out from beneath a paper-thin gown. His legs are foreign, skinny and hairless, smudged with dark spots and an impressive bruise that blooms against the harsh line of his shinbone. Old man legs, he realizes, and it strikes him that he must be ancient. Or, at least, much, much older than he feels.

"How old am I?" The words tumble out unbidden, and the voice that carries them croaks with age and disuse.

"You are seventy-two years young, Mr. Clark." She smiles as she says it, her voice so matter-of-fact it takes a moment for Mitch to grasp that she's talking about him.

"Seventy-two?" he repeats, wondering.

"Handsome as ever," she assures him.

"I need to shave," Mitch murmurs. It sounds strange, even to his ears. And especially so when he raises a hand to his chin and discovers that the folds of skin there are soft, creased with delicate pleats like a leaf of used crepe. These cheeks haven't felt the scrape of a razor in a very long time. But the compulsion is so vivid it's hard to shake. He can still feel his wife's palm on his cheek, her hand rigid and icy though she cupped his face in a parody of tenderness.

"My wife likes me clean-shaven," Mitch says, because it's the truth. Or it was the truth. He'd like to remember, but all he catches is a whiff of her spicy perfume, the hard line of disapproval that arcs around her mouth, and then she's gone.

The young woman in pink ignores him. "Would you like a bath this morning?"

It's a confounding question. A bath? Does he like baths? Do men take baths? Does Mitch take baths? He must, because she doesn't wait for an answer, just eases his hand to the cool railing of the bed where he teeters on the edge of the mattress. The nurse's aide creeps into the bathroom on silent feet, leaving him alone with the tangle of his thoughts. Soon he hears the sound of running water, the squeak of metal on metal as she adjusts the temperature.

For a second Mitch can almost feel the sting of scalding water on his skin. He's standing in a shower filled with steam and the bright, sharp scent of Irish Spring. The shower curtain is white, and beyond it he can see the rest of the house. He knows that he can't possibly be there, his body fit and sturdy instead of palsied and weak like it is now. But this waking dream seems more real to him than the aide and the hard bed with the stamped sheets.

Mitch closes his eyes, and in his mind he floats beyond the shower curtain and the walls of the avocado-colored bathroom where he loosened tight muscles with water so hot it made him look sunburnt, boiled. Through a carpeted hall, past a trio of bedrooms, down the stairs. The house is a split-level, the kitchen–living room combo sprawling across a generous main floor. But in spite of the wide-open space, it feels cramped to him. Tight and tinged with sorrow like the constricted wheeze of each laborious breath he now takes. It is not a safe place. Or a happy place. But he knows beyond a shadow of a doubt that once it was his home.

The house in his mind is thick with tension that emanates from the woman he called his wife. The memory of her hand still lingers on his face. It makes his skin tingle.

"Not too hot," the aide calls from the bathroom. Her words echo off the tile in the tiny room and call Mitch back to the present. "I know that you don't like your baths scalding."

I don't? Mitch sighs, extends a foot to the floor, and tests the waxed surface with a toe that looks so bent it must be arthritic. The cold nips his skin, leeches into his bones. A shiver wracks his body and makes him cough. But the tremor also shakes something loose: a heavy stone at the very bottom of his personal history, a place where the rubble of a ruined life has collected after the fallout of an explosion he can't recall.

Suddenly he remembers.

Everything.

It's a flash, a split second of technicolor brilliance that leaves him aching, a warm tear already sliding off his quivering jaw. But like smoke that lingers after the burst of fireworks in July, the shadows of his life cling in wisps of mist and memories. It's beautiful and terrible all at once.

t/sw666666s

"We're ready to go, Mr. Clark." The nurse startles him with her sudden presence, and Mitch gasps as if he has forgotten how to breathe.

"I . . ." but there is nothing he wants to say.

The aide's eyes are soft, her hands even more so when she reaches to take his elbow. "It's a special day," she tells him. "You don't want to miss breakfast. We always have pancakes on Christmas Eve."

Mitch shakes his head as if to rid it of the sights and scents that drift over him at the mention of Christmas. Apple cider, pine from the live tree he used to haul from the grocery store parking lot, the tang of sweat and snow that lingered around a pair of small boots waiting near the door. A child, he thinks, surprised. Something warm fills his chest. A girl, he realizes. A pair of pink boots.

"We're going to sing carols tonight." The aide smiles suddenly. "And guess what? It's snowing." She leaves him on the bed and goes to throw open the curtains that cover the only window in the small room.

When she slides back the heavy cloth, morning light spills into his bedroom and touches the tips of Mitch's feet with a cool swath of creamy white. The sky is dove gray, the clouds so high and far away the snowflakes that fill the window frame seem to be falling from heaven itself. And the snow is a blessing, drifting in clusters as big as cotton balls and softening the harsh landscape of a flat, midwestern field under a blanket so fresh and new Mitch wishes he could crawl beneath it.

"Isn't it pretty?" The aide sighs a little as she considers the transformation of the world before her, but Mitch can't bring himself to respond.

He isn't at The Heritage Home anymore, trapped in a room where he is surely living out the end of his days. Instead, he's squinting at the silhouette of a memory, watching it bloom with color and burst to life, a gorgeous, stolen moment that he clings to even as it begins to fade at the edges.

Mitch can see her so clearly it's hard not to believe that the clock has rewound. Her hair is woven in twin braids, a crooked attempt at elegance that is fuzzed with errant curls, pieces that have defied her careful handiwork. Somehow, this only adds to her childish beauty—the understanding that in lieu of a mother's tender ministrations, her own slender hands struggled to tame her locks. Her cheeks are flushed rose, her lips parted in the laughter of the young, her gaze flecked with the silver of a million stars reflected in her eyes. There are diamonds in her hair, and when she reaches for Mitch, he takes her cold hands in his own. He presses her fingers between his warm palms, wishes that he could hold her tight. For just a moment longer. Forever.

But she's already gone.

CHAPTER 1

RACHEL

October 1

"He's going to kill me."

"Oh, he is not. Don't be so melodramatic." Lily gave me a withering look and snapped a tight crease in the towel she was folding.

I watched my daughter add the neat hand towel to the growing pile of clean laundry, and found myself marveling again at the graceful curve of her neck, the spark in her denim-blue eyes. Lily was a wonder: smart and beautiful and spunky. But she was also wrong. If I followed through with our secret plan, Cyrus might very well kill me.

"He's going to be furious," I said.

Lily shrugged. "So? Stand up to him, Mom. What's the worst that could happen?"

I could think of a dozen different scenarios, and none of them were pleasant. But what did my eleven-year-old daughter know about the complexity of a sad and loveless marriage? How could I expect her to understand the give and take of my relationship with her father? I gave. Cyrus took. It was a simple equation. One that I knew by heart.

"It's complicated, sweetie." I tucked the final washcloth into a square and began loading the piles of linens into the laundry basket for distribution throughout the four bathrooms in our palatial house. We had more bathrooms than family members, but I considered the sprawl of our ungainly residence a blessing: It gave me many places to hide. Guest rooms and dark hallways. Sometimes closets. But Lily didn't know about any of that.

Cyrus and I only fought when our daughter was asleep, and though our confrontations usually consisted of nothing more than vicious words and savage insults, I couldn't stand the thought of her hearing the ugly things her father said to me. I had vowed long ago that Lily would never suffer the truth of my messed-up marriage, and I had kept my promise. I drew Cyrus away, made sure that there was never a reason for his anger to light upon our daughter. It worked. I was an exemplary lightning rod.

"Well," Lily put her hands on her narrow hips and arched her eyebrows at me, "I think you have to do it. Mr. Wever needs you. How can you say no?"

"I can't say no," I sighed. "I'll do it. But you have to promise me that you won't let it slip to Dad. It's our secret, right?"

Lily crossed her heart with a slender finger and fixed me with an impish grin. She was mature for her age, but the glint in her eye reminded me that my daughter was still a little girl—and one who thrilled at the mere thought of a secret. It struck me that her enthusiasm for my short-term assistance in Max Wever's tailor shop had more to do with the promise of intrigue than a selfless desire to help an elderly man in need. My heart broke a little at her unblemished view of life: Lily still believed in innocent secrets, the heady rush of a good mystery, and happily ever after. I wasn't about to disabuse her of those sweet notions. Little girls should be allowed to dream.

"You're going to miss the bus," I said, hoisting the laundry basket into my arms. I leaned forward and kissed the cheek that Lily proffered. "Remember: I want you to come straight to Eden after school."

Lily giggled. "That sounds so silly." She affected what I assumed to be a bad impersonation of my voice: "Come to Paradise after school, Lily." She dropped the phony inflection. "I can't believe Mr. Wever named his tailor shop Eden Custom Tailoring."

"It was my idea," I said. "A long time ago." A life-time ago.

"Subtle," Lily joked.

"How do you even know what subtle means?" I shook my head at her. "Be serious. I want you to come straight to the shop. But don't take the bus there, okay? Get off at your regular stop and then walk."

"Should I duck behind trees?" Lily struck a Charlie's Angel pose. "Double back to make sure no one is follow-ing me?"

"Now you're being melodramatic." I pursed my lips and tried not to regret my decision too much. "Just try to keep this under wraps, please? You have to believe me, Lil. Your dad would not be happy if he knew that I was going to help Max. He likes me home, you know that."

"I know." Lily grabbed her backpack off the table and slung it over her shoulders. "I'm a good secret keeper."

You're not the only one, I thought. And before I could further expound on the covert nature of my temporary appointment at Eden Custom Tailoring, Lily flounced out of the room. I heard the tap of her light footsteps in the entryway, and then the slam of the front door. It seemed symbolic to me, a final drumbeat that echoed through our cavernous house with finality. That signified an end.

But also a beginning. Because even though I was afraid to admit it, I felt like a door had been cracked in my soul.

It was a tiny opening, to be sure, but there was the hint of something new in the air, something unexpected.

I stifled a shiver, and shot up a prayer that Cyrus would never find out.

Max and Elena Wever saved me. I know that sounds sentimental, but I believe that it's true. My mother, the infamous Beverly Anne, died when I was fourteen years old, and in the swirling aftermath of anger and confusion, Max and Elena stepped in and pulled me from the wreckage.

Bev was killed when the family station wagon got up close and personal with an oak tree on a lazy summer Tuesday. The official police report stated that she lost control of her vehicle and careened off the road causing an untimely and fatal accident, but most of Everton knew the truth: Bev was drunk as a skunk at two o'clock in the afternoon, and was too busy reaching for a bottle of gin that had rolled under the seat to pay much attention to the hairpin curve that marked the very edge of town.

Years later, when one of Cyrus's chic friends mixed me a martini from the liquor cabinet in her posh kitchen, just the scent of vermouth and my mother's signature gin was enough to make me queasy. I swore off alcohol altogether.

To me it smelled of bitter words and anger and death. It smelled like my mother.

But before I knew what a martini was, before I could articulate the hurt and frustration that I felt at the mere mention of Bev's name, I was just a kid without a mom, and Max and Elena Wever saw the depth of my need and reached out.

Back then, Eden Custom Tailoring didn't even exist. Max and Elena were simply "the tailors" to the community of Everton, and they mended slacks and sewed custom suit jackets in their garage turned sewing shop. They lived next door to the split-level where I grew up, and though I knew who they were and what they did, I had never set foot in their workspace or even said hello to them until the day that Max stopped me on the sidewalk.

It was a hot, hazy afternoon in July, and my neighbor was dressed in black pants and a crisp, long-sleeved dress shirt with the cuffs rolled up to his elbows. I was sweating in a tank top and cut-off jean shorts, and too miserable from the heat and the fever of my own bewilderment at life to pay him any attention.

"Do you have good eyes?" Max asked me out of the blue as I walked past his driveway.

I turned and considered the man who was my neighbor. He was bent and grizzled, a stooping giant with hands like bear paws and tufts of wiry hair poking from his ears like forgotten bits of cotton. I wasn't afraid of him, but we had never talked before, and as soon as he inquired after my optical health I was convinced that there was good reason we avoided each other: He obviously had dementia. Most people regarded me with thinly veiled pity and apologized immediately about the loss of my mother. Max skipped right over these trivialities.

"My eyes are fine," I told him. Then I spun on my heel and kept walking—I decided it was best not to encourage him. But his next question stopped me in my tracks.

"Would you like a job?"

A job? In the month after my mother's death my life had consisted of little more than parrying people's unwelcome condolences and trying to weed out the sincere offers of help from the ones that were born of avarice and gossip. It seemed everyone wanted to know what had gone on in the Clark house, and there was no lack of scandalmongers willing and eager to rifle through our home in an effort to ascertain the truth. But Mr. Wever's question was singular, unexpected. I couldn't have ignored him if I wanted to.

"What kind of a job?" I asked warily.

"My wife and I are tailors," he told me in his thick Dutch accent. "We mend clothes. Make new ones."

As if I didn't know.

"We could use someone to sew buttonholes, press fabrics, run errands . . ."

"I'd be a gofer?"

Mr. Wever looked confused.

"An errand girl," I clarified, not entirely put off by the thought. Anything sounded better than wandering the streets of Everton with nothing to do and nowhere to go, the tragedy of my mother's demise following me like the proverbial ball and chain.

"Yes," Mr. Wever said slowly. "An errand girl, I suppose. But maybe more than that. If you have good eyes." He took a shuffling step toward me, and I lifted my chin as if offering up my eyes for inspection. They were blue and bottomless, too big if I chose to believe my late mother's persistent criticism. And maybe my baby blues were a smidgen buggy, but I never understood why Bev felt the need to critique. They were her eyes, after all. I was the spitting image of my mother from the tips of my delicate fingers to the roots of my unruly ginger hair.

"How much?" I asked.

Mr. Wever hooked a finger around the wire frame of the glasses that were perched on his nose and tugged them down so he could regard me through the lower lens of his bifocals. His gaze was direct, and maybe just a little amused. "Three dollars an hour," he said. "The hours will change. Sometimes we will have a lot of work for you. Sometimes not."

Three dollars was less than minimum wage, but the

hours sounded suitably vague and variable. "Okay," I said, shrugging. "I'll be your errand girl."

Mr. Wever nodded once and gave me an earnest, tight-lipped smile. When he took a step toward me, I thought that he was going to rattle off a collection of do's and don'ts, an indomitable checklist for working in his hallowed shop. But instead, he extended his hand and waited patiently for me to reciprocate. Our handshake was solemn, and as my fingers disappeared into his giant palm, I realized that we were sealing a covenant.

"Elena and I look forward to seeing you tomorrow morning at eight," he said.

Since Bev's death I had gotten used to loafing, but Mr. Wever didn't really leave room for discussion on the matter of my starting time. I lifted a shoulder and he must have taken the gesture as assent because he nodded again and turned to go. "Thank you," I called after him.

He was shuffling up the driveway, and he only acknowledged my gratitude by waving his hand in the air as if he was swatting at a cloud of gnats.

"I'll see you tomorrow, Mr. Wever," I added.

"Max."

"What?"

"Call me Max!" he shouted. And then he disappeared into the side door of his attached garage.

I worked for Max and Elena for just over five years. At

first, I swept the floor, wound spools of thread, and answered the telephone when they had straight pins sticking from between their lips. When Max discovered that I was a hard worker and a quick study, he taught me to starch and press the trousers so that the thick pleat would stand like a narrow ridge. It was fine work, but I didn't truly fall in love with it until Elena made her first wedding dress, a hand-spun creation for a young woman in her church who couldn't afford a store-bought gown.

The tailor shop was forever transformed for me when Elena purchased an extravagant bolt of Italian Silk Mikado. It was insanely expensive, but the dress was going to be a gift, and Elena took gift-giving very seriously. The day that the fabric arrived from Milan, I stayed late after Max retired from the workroom. Elena and I carefully pushed aside the heavy wools, herringbones, and tweeds that would soon clothe the men of Everton and lifted the surprisingly heavy box onto the table. Then Elena brought out the silk, and we unrolled it across the surface of the wide worktable, stunned by the way that it gleamed and danced in the light.

"I may never sew a pair of pants again." Elena laughed.

But of course she did.

However, at least once or twice a year, Elena would leave the tailoring to her husband and indulge in her favorite hobby: dressmaking. As for me, I looked forward to those forays into the world of satin and lace with an almost frantic excitement. And yet, I couldn't complain about sewing men's suits. There was something uniquely warm and comforting about helping Max get the symmetry and alignment of the pinstripes on a custom suit jacket just perfect. It was fun and foreign. Decidedly masculine.

My dad rarely wore a suit. And the one he hauled out for special occassions was a relic. His closet was filled with Wrangler jeans and whatever shirt he could buy for ten dollars or less at Bomgaars. I never really thought of my dad's clothes until I started making suits with Max. All at once my dad's workingman's wardrobe seemed cheap and tasteless, the uniform of a man who always had dirt under his fingernails and a sunburn peeling the skin of his nose. I didn't mean to be shallow, but I found myself wishing that my dad would take himself a bit more seriously.

" 'Clothes make the man,' " Max would quote, eyeing me sidelong before he finished: " 'Naked people have little or no influence on society.' "

"Mark Twain." I'd laugh. "But it's a silly quote."

"No, it's a true quote." He'd crinkle up his eyes, thinking. "How about: 'If honor be your clothing, the suit will last a lifetime; but if clothing be your honor, it will soon be worn threadbare.' "

"I've never heard that one before."

"William Arnot. He was a preacher. Knew what he was talking about."

I pursed my lips. "It's a nice saying, Max. But I think it undermines what we're doing here. Aren't we making clothing?"

"It's a balance, honey. That's what I want you to understand. As much as people would like to believe otherwise, how we present ourselves on the outside reveals something about who we are on the inside. I don't have to wear a three-piece suit to be a good person, but I would like everything about me—even my clothes—to reflect a certain uncompromising integrity."

"Is that why you make suits?"

Max laughed. "I make suits because my father made suits. And his father before him. What do you think Wever means in Dutch? It's all I know how to do. However, since I make suits, they're going to be excellent in every way. The best possible quality."

"Because you are a man of uncompromising integrity."

"I hope so," Max murmured with a wry smile. "I sure do try."

They both tried, Max and Elena, and I adored them. Though we never talked about it, for all intents and purposes, I was the daughter they never had. I always wondered if Max and Elena left a child in Dutch soil, or if they were simply never able to conceive. But I didn't question their love for me, and for a few years at least I grew up grateful that my surrogate family accepted me, flaws, baggage, and all—especially when my real family didn't. Especially because I didn't really have a family. Before I was old enough to drive a car, I was more or less an orphan: Bev was dead and my father pretended I was. Or, at least, I felt like he did.

"We are not 'the tailor shop' anymore," Max said the day that Elena and I finished our tenth wedding dress. He surveyed the soft, lovely fabrics that seemed to bloom in unexpected bursts from every corner of his formerly masculine garage. Poplin and seersucker and linen existed side by side with gauzy material that pooled and flowed like melted ice.

"Come now," Elena protested. "We'll always be 'the tailor shop.'" She leaned against him and kissed his wrinkled cheek placatingly.

"But we're more. We're . . ." Max's forehead wrinkled as if he was confused by what his store had become. "We're a dress shop, too."

Elena shook her head. "Not just any dress shop. A wedding dress shop."

"A bridal shop," I offered.

Max pretended to shiver and threw up his hands in defeat. "Women! I am surrounded!" He shook his head as he left the garage, but I caught the hint of a smile tugging at the corners of his lips.

"He'll be just fine," Elena assured me with a wink.

"Wounded pride is rarely fatal. As for us, I think it's time we gave this suit shop/tailor shop/bridal shop a name. A way for people to find us."

"Eden," I said without pause.

"Eden?"

"You know," I fumbled, "because it's perfect. Happy and new. Filled with possibility . . ." I trailed off.

Elena nodded slowly and I could practically see the wheels spinning behind her deep brown eyes. "Eden Custom Tailoring—so that there's room for the odd dress or two amid the army of suits. I think it'll work."

Of course it would work. Everyone needed a little reminder of something whole and full of promise. Everyone needed a bit of paradise.

Especially people who sometimes felt like their lives were anything but.

Eden Custom Tailoring became a cult phenomenon when the youth of Everton graduated from high school and fled their tiny hometown. As Everton natives populated LA, Chicago, New York, and beyond, sooner or later they found that special someone and remembered the old couple that sewed exclusive suits and wedding dresses back in their all-but-forgotten hometown. Calls started coming in for gowns of Duchess silk and Italian satin, and accompanying those extravagant orders came the imperious directive: "It must be perfect." Which translated into: "We have no budget."

Max bought an old photography studio on Main Street, which he transformed into a charming shop with a custom fitting room and a five-sided mirror with a two-foot pedestal. It worked well when Max had to carefully measure the distinguished gentlemen of Everton, but the brides were the customers who appreciated the pedestal the most. The young women loved to preen and admire themselves from every possible angle. The lighting was dim and flattering since there were no windows in the shop, and though that fact had seemed like a liability when Max first purchased the building, it turned out to be a boon: Most brides were thrilled that their unique creation would remain a mystery until their stirring walk down the aisle.

And brides-to-be weren't the only ones who were happy that Eden Custom Tailoring was a dark, nondescript structure on a quiet corner in Everton. As I gripped the handle of the back door and cast a furtive glance over my shoulder to make sure that no one was watching my entrance, I silently blessed Max for forgoing a bright, public building with views of our historic downtown. If he had opted for accessibility and pizzazz, I would never have been able to say yes to his harried call for help.

Satisfied that the shadowy alley behind Eden Custom Tailoring was empty, I quickly opened the steel door and slipped inside. The back room hadn't changed much in the twelve years since I quit working for Max and Elena. It was still filled with boxes from exotic locales all over the world, and hanging from metal rods along two walls of the small space were dozens of hangers draped with fabrics in every shade and hue. A muted breath escaped my lips and I resisted the urge to take the nearest length of organza in my fingers. But rather than risk spoiling the fabric with the oils on my palm, I ran the back of my wrist against the lovely cloth and marveled at the way it felt like water against my skin.

"It's pretty, isn't it?"

Max was standing in the doorway between the back room and the workshop, his crest of snowy hair almost touching the top of the frame. In spite of his height, he seemed diminished to me, smaller somehow since the last time I saw him up close. "I don't know what to do with her fabric now that she's gone . . ." he said, trailing off almost apologetically.

I thought I could hold myself together, but at the sight of him I was undone. A sob cut loose from my throat, and before I could contain it there was a torrent of tears to match.

"Oh, Rachel." Max held out his hands to me and I came to him, careful not to bowl him over in my desperation to feel his arms around me. He tucked me close carefully. Wordlessly. There was nothing we could say.

"I'm so sorry," I finally managed after several minutes, my face pressed against his shoulder.

"For what?"

"For not coming sooner. I wanted to go to Elena's funeral," I gasped, horrified that I had let them put her in the ground without saying good-bye. I tried to explain, more for my own sake than his: "Cyrus had a work thing and—"

"It's okay," Max said.

But it wasn't okay. It wasn't even close to being okay. "I should have been there."

"You're here now."

You're here now. His words seemed to echo through the empty space that Elena's death had hewn in my soul. But maybe the fissure had happened long before that. Maybe it began with Bev, and was deepened by the silence of my cowardly father. Maybe Cyrus carved it further still, creating a cavern that resounded with accusations, allegations that piled up against me: You're weak. You're ugly. You're stupid and unlovable and worthless.

Maybe Bev was right all those years ago and Cyrus's

continuation of her hurtful monologue was perfectly be-
fitting for someone as cheap and useless as me. Maybe
I was all the things they said I was. But standing in the
warm circle of Max's arms, I was something else, too.

"You're right," I said. "I'm here now."

It was a start.

CHAPTER 2

RACHEL

October 1

Lily appeared in the back room at Eden Custom Tailoring precisely at three-thirty, wearing a grin she tried hard to conceal and carrying a perfect red maple leaf between her thumb and forefinger. "Wow," she breathed, taking in the swaths of bolted cloth and the fresh, clean scent of the place.

"Don't touch anything," I said. I buried my nose in the mug of coffee I was drinking and squeezed my tired eyes shut. "If you'd like I can give you some scraps later and teach you how to do a running stitch."

"Really?" Lily sounded ecstatic at the thought.

"Sure, honey. You'll just have to leave it here. We can't risk taking any fabric home." After a long, peaceful day in Max's shop, those words seemed almost ridiculous to me. I shook my head to clear it. "How was your day?"

Lily drooped her shoulders and let her backpack slide to the floor. She kicked it into an empty corner of the narrow room, never once taking her eyes off the bolts of fabric that hung all around her and hemmed her in. "Fine," she said absently. "Oh." She looked at the leaf in her hand, remembering. "I found this for you. It's perfect, isn't it?"

I took the stem of the leaf between my fingers and twirled it in front of my face. The five spires were precisely serrated, each tiny tip sharp as if it had been die-cut with a brand new press. Best of all, the leaf was entirely uniform, the same deep, cardinal color from the firm spire of the stem to the delicate, papery edges. "It's beautiful." I smiled, loving my daughter for her ability to find treasure all around her.

From the time she was old enough to toddle, Lily was always bringing me things: first dandelions that had been mashed in her chubby fist, then prickly pinecones and rocks shot through with quartz. I thought she'd grow out of it, but she had an eye for hidden things, and the gems she uncovered now were truly unique. I had her little gifts secreted all over the house. Flowers preserved between the pages of my favorite books, iridescent snail shells scattered in my jewelry box, round stones as smooth and polished as marbles in the pockets of my coat where I could slip my hand inside and touch them. Each offering seemed like a little piece of Lily.

"Thank you," I said.

"Where's Mr. Wever?"

"In the workroom. I was taking a break. Waiting for you."

Lily glanced at the watch on her wrist. "We've got to be home in one hour. You'd better get back to work!"

"Just one hour? You sound like my Fairy Godmother. When the clock strikes four-thirty . . ."

Lily laughed. "I guess that makes you Cinderella."

"Hardly." I winked at her and downed the dregs of my coffee. "Grab your books. Max and I have cleared off a space for you to do your homework."

"Homework?" Lily crinkled up her nose. "I want to help."

"Homework first. That's our routine at home and we have to stick to it."

Lily pursed her lips like she was going to argue, but my warning look was enough to stop her protestations. She sighed and lifted a stack of textbooks from her bag, then followed me through the doorway into the spacious workroom.

At the sound of our footsteps, Max looked up from the table where he was hemming a pair of men's pants out of pewter-colored wool. While Elena had slowly worked on her unique wedding dresses, over the years Max continued to create men's suits that rivaled Armani. In fact, he had made such a name for himself that a chain of three specialty shops in New York, Chicago, and LA had commissioned him to create a custom line. Not only were Eden suits in great demand, they were a mark of prestige and good taste.

Something lodged in my throat at the sight of him bowed over the work that had earned this simple man a name in places he had never even thought to visit. His humility, his lack of pretension in spite of all he had accomplished amazed me. I swallowed, managed to say: "Max, I'd like you to meet my daughter, Lily."

He straightened up slowly and readjusted the bifocals that had slid precariously close to the tip of his hooked nose. Though his stature and high, Dutch cheekbones made him seem intimidating, the moment Max smiled, the room was filled with warmth.

"So this is our girl," he said softly. And then he came around the table and took Lily's shoulders in his massive hands so he could study her sweet face.

I expected Lily to pull back, but instead she grinned at Max and gave him a quick, uncharacteristic hug around the middle. "Mom says you were kind of like her dad, so I guess that makes you kind of like my grandpa."

Guilt stabbed through me at the implications of her words: It wasn't fair that Lily had grown up without a grandfather in her life. But how could I have possibly remedied that? Cyrus's dad died when Lily was only two, and I hadn't spoken to my own father in years.

My father. Just the thought of him was enough to fill me with regret. Although our relationship had deteriorated by the time Cyrus entered my life, I was ashamed that I had allowed my husband to sever the final ties that held me to my dad. But what choice did I have? My father wasn't the only one I lost when I married Cyrus Price.

"You already have a grandfather," Max told Lily seriously. He gave me an indecipherable look. "Your grandpa was a hard worker and a good man. He always tried to provide for his family—"

"It's complicated," I interrupted briskly. Though I had spent my teenage years considering Max and Elena my family, they never let me forget that I had a father. A living, breathing dad of my own who just happened to be so caught up in his own life that he didn't have any time to acknowledge the fact that he had a daughter. A living, breathing daughter who needed a daddy. "I haven't seen my dad in years," I said breezily, even though I almost choked on the words. I haven't seen my dad in years . . .

and it broke my heart in so many pieces I wondered if it would ever be whole again.

"That's a terrible shame." Max frowned. The reproach in his voice made me cringe.

If Lily noticed the tension in the room, it didn't seem to faze her. "Well, Mr. Wever, it's nice to meet you all the same."

"Nice to meet you, too," he said, turning back to her with a smile. "And I'd love to be one of your grandfathers. You can never have too many grandpas, can you?"

Lily shook her head, grinning at the bear of a man before her. "I just wish I would have known you when I was a kid."

"You are a kid!" He laughed. "A peanut! A little goose."

I fumbled for words as I watched Lily and Max. The sight of them together made me realize just how lonely I was. How isolated and bitter my life had become. It took my breath away to see my daughter so light and happy, to realize that she needed a man in her life—the sort of man that her father couldn't be. "I'm sorry," I finally said, anguished by all the years that we had lost. All the years that Max and Elena could have been a part of our lives. "I should have—"

"Nonsense," Max broke in firmly. "Should is a terrible word."

"But—"

"But nothing. Life is a journey, Rachel. As you walk along the road you can either look back or you can look ahead." He stretched a single, crooked finger right past Lily's nose, and pointed to some faraway future that I couldn't begin to envision.

Lily squinted, following the line of Max's finger as if she couldn't wait to see what was in store. "Look ahead?" she guessed.

"You've got it, honey." Max gave her a wide smile. "Always look for the very next step."

Ten suits. Two months. Twenty thousand dollars. Those were the figures that Max presented to me when he called. I was so taken by the sound of his voice after all the years between us that I was rendered speechless—though he probably assumed I was experiencing sticker shock at the current price tag of just one of his suits.

"I hate to ask you, Rachel," Max had all but whispered. Cyrus was gone for the day, but there was a certain hushed quality to our conversation all the same. "It's just that it's too late to back out of this contract. I've already made the shipments to LA and Chicago, but the New York store is expecting my completed order by Christmas."

Hearing Max speak was like rewinding the clock, going back to a time in my life when things were simpler. Safer. I closed my eyes and listened to the sound of his breathing on the telephone line, and forgot to respond at all.

"It usually takes me two weeks to finish a suit. I'll never get them done on my own," Max continued. Then, softer: "Her heart attack was so unexpected. How could we have known? Elena was always so healthy. But now . . ." he trailed off. "What am I going to do, Rachel?"

"I'll help you," I said. Instantly I regretted it. How could I help him? Cyrus would never let me. But just as quickly as I rejected the idea, I embraced it again. "I'll help you," I forced myself to repeat. "At least, I'll try. If I can find a way to come, I'll be at your shop on Monday."

"Thank you," Max said.

"Don't thank me yet. I haven't promised anything. Besides, I haven't touched a needle in over a decade."

"It's like riding a bike," he assured me, his words light with hope. "I still remember the first time you tried a stitch. You were a natural."

But there was no way Max could remember the first time I picked up a sewing needle. He wasn't there.

From the ages of seven to ten, I wore the same Easter dress three years in a row. It wasn't that we were terribly poor, though we certainly weren't rich. Instead, the reason I had to squeeze into the same dress for several years running was that Bev liked to spend her money on things she could consume. And even if she had offered to take me to the mall, I wouldn't have gone with her for love or money. I couldn't stand the thought of anyone seeing me with her as she stumbled through the aisles at JC Penney.

Fortunately, it was a pretty dress. Blue, like my eyes, with a drop waist and a row of faux mother-of-pearl buttons that ran a dainty line from the top of the skirt all the way up to a lace collar. When I slid it over my head on Easter morning for the third time, I wasn't so much ashamed of the dress as I was ashamed of the way that it pulled tight across my shoulders and skimmed the tops of my knees instead of falling to my calves like it was supposed to. At ten years old, I was no fashionista, but I could tell when something didn't look right. And staring at myself in the mirror, I knew that I didn't look right.

Bev called me all manner of hurtful things from bucktoothed to stupid to an accident. But the name that stung the most was ugly, and as I considered the way I was squeezed into a too-tight, outdated dress I believed that what my mother said was true. I was ugly.

I had learned long ago that crying didn't do me a lick

of good, but I couldn't stop the hot tears that pricked at the corners of my eyes. Dad expected me to wear a dress to church, or I would have simply given up the blue dress for a pair of pants and a nice top, but he was strict about some things and Easter Sunday attire was one of them. He was waiting for me downstairs, probably checking his watch to make sure I wouldn't make him late.

Wiping at my eyes, I gritted my teeth and told myself that I didn't care what anyone thought of me. I didn't care that they knew my mother was a drunk, or that they called me Orphan Annie behind my back. My red hair and shabby clothes made me an easy target, but I decided I wouldn't give anyone the satisfaction of knowing that their teasing got to me. I took a deep breath and tried to ease an extra inch out of the fabric by giving the dress a good hard tug—and sent a handful of the ivory buttons flying in every direction.

Dad found me scrambling across my bedroom floor, trying to rescue buttons from their hiding places in dark corners and underneath the bed.

"What are you doing?" he asked, leaning in the doorway. He took up the entire space, his broad shoulders nearly touching the doorjamb on either side. Dad wasn't yet wearing his suit coat, and the defined muscles in his arms pressed against the fabric of his dress shirt.

"Nothing," I muttered, biting back tears.

"We have to get to church, Rach. We're going to be late."

"I know!" I half-shouted, turning to him from where I crouched on the floor. I had the top of my dress clutched in one hand, my fingers holding together the places where the missing buttons gaped to reveal my cotton slip.

"What in the world are you doing?" He took a step into the room, his brow furrowed in confusion or anger, I couldn't tell.

"I tore my dress," I said into my chest. "I have to wear pants this morning."

Dad loomed over me, his shadow blocking the glow from the ceiling light. "What do you mean you tore your dress?"

I offered up a handful of buttons, and Dad used the opportunity to pull me to my feet. He lifted me up as if I weighed nothing at all. "Some of the buttons popped off," I said. "The dress is too small."

"Nonsense." Dad put his finger under my chin and tipped my face so I was looking at him. If he noticed the tears in my eyes, he didn't say anything. "This dress fits you just fine. We just need to sew the buttons back on."

"No, Dad. Please. Just let me wear pants."

"On Easter? I don't think so, Rachel. Your mother is

even coming to church this morning. I want us all there together in our Sunday best. Maybe we'll even take a family picture."

I groaned. "Please, Dad. Just let me—"

"No." His tone left no room for discussion. "I want you to wear the dress."

I meekly slid off the ruined dress and accepted the bathrobe he offered me. Then Dad dragged me along as he went to hunt down an emergency sewing kit. We both knew that Bev would have no idea how to use it, so when we finally located the small, folded bundle at the back of the medicine cabinet Dad threaded the needle and handed it to me.

"I don't know how to sew a button on," I said, holding the slip of steel between my fingers gingerly.

He looked stunned for a moment. "You don't?"

"No."

"It can't be that hard." Dad glanced at his watch and gave me a pointed look. "We need to leave in less than ten minutes. Your mother is just finishing up her makeup."

Bev could spend the better part of an hour finishing up her makeup, but Dad was tapping his foot as if to remind me that the clock was ticking down. So, since I didn't know what else to do, I took hold of the fabric and stabbed the needle through the spot where the first button had left behind a frayed tail of white thread. It wasn't easy, but I looped the needle through the hole in the back of the tiny button and sunk it into the fabric again. I made four passes before the sharp point missed the intended target and pricked the tip of my index finger.

It didn't hurt that much, but I burst into tears all the same. "Please, Dad," I begged, my voice cracking. "Just let me wear pants!"

He took the dress from me and reached for my injured hand, but I had already stuck my finger in my mouth and I refused to let him look at it. "The blue matches your eyes," he said almost absently, fingering the cloth. And then he plucked the needle where it dangled from the end of a long thread and began to sew the button on himself.

I stood there, crying silently, and watched him sew every one of those six severed buttons back onto a dress that was two sizes too small. His fingers were thick and clumsy, and he swore under his breath once or twice, but he eventually finished the job. When he presented me with that horrible blue dress, it was wrinkled from the sweat of his calloused hands and discolored in spots. It looked like a used rag to me. Worst of all, what had once been a neat row of pretty buttons was now limp and uneven. The buttons sagged in some places and were stitched too tight to the cheap cloth in others.

Dad didn't seem to get it. He didn't even realize that his handiwork fell horribly short. "I'll go find your mother," he said. "If you get dressed quickly, we can make it before anyone notices we're late."

I put on the dress, but as I carefully slipped each crooked button through its hole, I decided that my father didn't understand me. It felt like he didn't even try. And that stung more than the wicked whispers of the girls who made fun of my dress.

CHAPTER 3

MITCH

December 24, 8:00 A.M.

The dining room of The Heritage Home is brightly lit and filled with people. But in spite of the crowd and the appearance of bustle, it is unusually peaceful. Clusters of elderly men and women huddle at an assortment of mismatched tables, whispering to each other as if age has simply erased the need to be loud. There is a small pot with a red poinsettia in the center of every table, and Christmas music hovers over everything like a mist. Best of all, the scent of griddle-hot butter and warm syrup fills the air. Pancakes? Mitch wonders. He loves pancakes.

It is not an unhappy place, but Mitch pauses in the doorway of the large room for a moment and glances around timidly. The tables are arranged with space for wheelchairs and walkers to manuever between them, and Mitch is filled with a quick gratitude that he can still walk on his own two feet. But he doesn't know where to go. There are no place markers on the tables that he can see, and no one looks familiar. He swallows down a wave of loneliness and tries to resist the urge to go back to the strange room that suddenly feels like home. However, just as he is about to tell the nurse's aide he's not in the mood for breakfast, he catches a glimpse of a man aross the room.

He is tall and narrow, almost elegant, and something about the steady way that he carries himself makes him look like he doesn't belong in an old folks' home. Mitch watches as the composed man carefully lowers himself into one of four chairs at an empty table. Then the gentleman reaches a tapered hand for the linen napkin before him and unfurls it in one graceful snap. The fabric drifts lightly to his lap, and the old man watches it as if the secrets of the universe are written on the starched folds. He closes his eyes. Sighs.

"I want to sit there," Mitch says, pointing to the man.

"It's not your usual table," the nurse's aide chirps. She has a grip on his elbow and Mitch wiggles his arm loose with an attempt at a grouchy snort. "Whatever you'd like,

Mr. Clark," she amends, and though she should look chastened, Mitch is disappointed to see that the young lady is only amused. He decides he must work on his grumpy old man routine.

"I can seat myself," Mitch says, and he takes off without a backward glance. He crosses the dining room with what he would like to believe is a certain contemptuous dignity.

When he arrives at the small, round table, the unfamiliar gentleman is still gazing at his lap. "Is this seat taken?" Mitch asks, putting his hand on the back of the chair across from the stranger.

"Are we friends today, Mitch?" The man looks up and fixes Mitch with a gentle half-smile.

"Excuse me?" Mitch can't help staring. He tries unsuccessfully to place the man's bright blue eyes, his strong chin. "Do I know you?"

The man shakes his head, adjusts his smile. "I've seen you around," he says vaguely. "My name is Cooper."

"Nice to meet you," Mitch says, but all at once he wonders if they've met somewhere before. "Care if I join you?"

"Certainly not," Cooper says.

There is a long moment of silence as Mitch settles into his seat. He puts his napkin on his lap, trying to mimic the flourish with which Cooper performed the same action. But Mitch's hands are clumsy; he feels like he is all thumbs. In the end he leaves the linen balled up and reaches for the utensils that frame his place setting. He is stunned to find that there are four pieces of indecipherable silverware. He glares at them, trying to focus, to make the gleaming silver make sense, but he doesn't know what they are for.

"You won't need your spoon this morning," Cooper says kindly, picking up the utensil with the shallow bowl. "Not unless you want your pancakes pureed." He leans forward and peers closely at Mitch. "Nope. Looks like you've still got your teeth."

Mitch doesn't quite know how to take Cooper's teasing, but he picks up his spoon and sets it off to the side.

"And I don't know why they give us two forks. It's not like they'll be serving salad with breakfast." Cooper lifts the smaller fork and adds it to his discard pile. "There. All you need is a fork and a knife."

Fork. Knife. Mitch remembers now. One for each hand. He wonders if he still knows how to use them.

"Pancakes today," Cooper says conversationally. "They make the batter from scratch with fresh buttermilk. A nice Christmas tradition."

"It's Christmas?"

"Not today. Tomorrow. But there's something extra special about Christmas Eve, don't you think? It's all about the anticipation—the hope of what's to come."

Mitch doesn't really know if Christmas Eve is all that

special, or even what he would hope for if the holiday is all about expectation like Cooper says. But Cooper's words have stirred something just beneath the surface, and all at once Mitch is overcome with a longing that he can't describe. He wants something, wants it desperately, but he can't remember what it is. It's as if he's been waiting for so long that he's forgotten exactly what it is he's been waiting for.

Mitch's stomach growls. Maybe he's just hungry. Maybe he's been waiting for pancakes.

"My wife used to work at a truck stop," Mitch says, surprising himself with the unanticipated memory. "She made the most amazing buttermilk pancakes."

"I remember them." Cooper smiles. "That was back in the day when no one blinked an eye if you melted an entire stick of butter on your stack of flapjacks. Real butter. Not that fake margarine stuff."

Mitch can almost see the golden domes of sweet whole cream butter. They looked like tiny scoops of ice cream that left a warm trail across the surface of crisp-edged cakes. He returns Cooper's smile. "Gorgeous."

"Well, I've never heard anyone call a pancake gorgeous, but okay." Cooper shrugs.

"Not the pancakes." Mitch's laugh is more like a cough, but at least it's genuine. "The woman. She was a beautiful woman."

Cooper nods, but his eyes seem flat. "She was definitely pretty."

"You know my wife?"

"Knew," Cooper says tenderly. "She's been gone for a long time, Mitch."

Mitch crumples the fabric of his pants in his sweaty palms. Of course, he knew that. He knew she was gone. But for just a moment he could see her. Slim hips beneath a white apron, eyes that sparked with fire and ice. She had a tongue on her, but Mitch couldn't really tell you what that meant. He battles a vague sense of discomfort, a wave of quiet shame that makes him both love and loathe the woman who stands at the very edge of his broken memory.

All at once Mitch feels like he might cry. It's a startling revelation, a feeling that he fights because there is something inside him that knows men are not supposed to cry. He knows he is not supposed to cry. There are old callouses on his hands, scars that line his arms and testify to the fact that he is—was—a man's man. The sort of man who would scoff at tears. Mitch blinks hard, clears his throat.

"What do you remember about your wife?" Cooper prods lightly.

"She had lovely hands." Mitch's mouth curves at the

thought of her slender fingers. "She wore her hair back when she waitressed, and earrings that dangled down her long neck. She had a great laugh."

"That she did."

Mitch frowned. "But she didn't laugh often."

"Why not?"

"She couldn't. Someone stole her joy." Mitch knows that it's true, even though he can't explain why or what happened to make his wife such a paradox. She was beautiful and cruel. Broken and harsh. He can feel the hurt radiate off her, a sparking, vicious energy like a current of electricity. To touch her was to expose yourself to the sting of a live wire.

"She was sad," Mitch says.

"Why?"

"She was hurt." His hands tighten into fists in his lap. "How anyone could ever hurt a child . . ." he can't bring himself to finish.

"It's beyond comprehension," Cooper says quietly.

"No one really understood her."

"Did you understand her?" Cooper asks.

"I don't know. But I think I loved her."

"I think you did, too."

"She did bad things," Mitch whispers.

"I know," Cooper says.

"And I loved her all the same." Mitch takes a shaky breath. "Was that wrong of me?"

Cooper leans across the table and Mitch is amazed to realize that his eyes are not the only ones that sparkle with unshed tears. "Of course it wasn't wrong of you. Everyone deserves to be loved."

CHAPTER 4

RACHEL

October 8

My father once told me that we are powerless against the people we love.

I think he was trying to help his nine-year-old daughter understand why he loved the woman who had just passed out on our living room couch, but the lesson was lost on me at the time. I didn't get it that he had no choice but to brush her hair back from her pale cheek and tuck a blanket around her arms with a tenderness that made my breath catch. He wasn't doing it out of obligation—he was caring for her because it was all his heart knew how to do. My father was defenseless against my mother.

What did I know about that sort of vulnerability?
About being completely laid bare before another person?
I didn't understand that sort of love until the day that Lily
was born. As I marveled at her tiny fingers, the fresh-from-
God scent of her skin, I knew that loving her was what I
was created to do. In a way, I lost myself in that moment.
But it didn't matter. She mattered.

Although I gave myself over to all sorts of indignity and
recklessness in my love for my daughter, the thought of
losing control in any other area of my life left me with a
hollow pit in my stomach. After just one week of working in secret with Max, my stomach was in knots and my
blood pressure was undoubtedly through the roof. But
though my clandestine job was utter foolishness, I couldn't
have gone back on my promise if I wanted to. I loved Max,
and while he ministered to me during the long hours we
spent together in his shop, for one of the few times in my
life I felt certain that I was ministering to him, too. It was
a heady feeling.

Yet, as much as I adored our time together, five measly
work days assured me that the game I was playing was a
dangerous one. My life was simply too ordered to withstand the sort of chaos that came hand in hand with de-
ceiving my husband.

To say that I was a creature of habit would be more
than a bit of an understatement. For more years than I

could remember, I did the same thing in the same way day after day after day. My coffeepot started to perk at six o'clock. I woke to an internal alarm clock, crept out of bed so I didn't disturb Cyrus, and showered in the downstairs bathroom—the one with the robin's-egg-blue paint and white wainscoting that reminded me of a beach house. Though I kept my shower short, it was a few minutes of reprieve, a place where I could pretend that I lived the sort of life where a beach vacation with my family was a sweet and precious memory instead of something I tried to forget. But it was a fantasy. The truth was, I did my best to erase the week that we spent in Florida when Lily turned eight.

When Cyrus announced that we were taking a family vacation, I was stunned. He was well versed in solo trips with his friends—pheasant hunting expeditions into the heart of South Dakota, snowmobiling weekends to secluded corners of Wyoming, and even the occasional jaunt to Las Vegas for business—but we hadn't attempted a holiday together since our pathetic stab at a second honeymoon on our fifth wedding anniversary. Florida with just the three of us sounded like a second chance to me. I tried to conjure up images of us laughing together, shelling on Sanibel Island or licking ice cream cones as we window-shopped in Naples. The pictures were fuzzy and indistinct, but if I imagined really hard I could make myself believe that Cyrus wanted that happy,

postcard-worthy family, too. I could make myself believe
that things were about to change. That they were going to
go back to the way they had been.

There was a time when we were in love. Truly, madly,
deeply. Like every story worth its salt. Cyrus was handsome and rugged, the sort of man who embodied every
masculine stereotype and cliché. He could be prickly and
gruff, but then, who would ever want to soften his rough
edges? I didn't care if Cyrus was a bit of a rogue, because
he adored me. He treated me like a princess in need of
rescue, and I complied because, quite simply, I loved being
rescued by him.

A family vacation to Florida sounded like nothing so
much as a daring rescue mission. Surely Cyrus had sug-
gested the unexpected holiday as a way to sweep me off
my feet. As a way to make up for all the time we had lost.

Of course, my daydreams were dashed. All Cyrus
wanted to do was lie by the pool at our resort and watch
the college girls who lounged at the edge of the water in
bikinis made from scraps of cloth. He spent most of the
week with his sunglasses on, eyes half-mast, but I knew
what he was looking at—anything and everything but
me, his wife of eleven years, the woman who bore him a
daughter and had the nasty, emergency C-section scar to
prove it. But, I suppose, who could blame him? My freckles
came out in the sun, and my milky pale skin blushed pink

even beneath SPF 50. And next to those strapless, slinky suits, my plain, black one-piece looked like a nun's habit. I wasn't surprised when Cyrus started going to the clubhouse to "hang out with the guys" after Lily was tucked in bed.

But in spite of our failed family vacation, I still loved the beach-themed bathroom in our house. And for half an hour in the early morning before everyone else woke up, it was my sea-blue haven. A place where I could stand in the swirling, hot steam from my shower and put on the predictable uniform that would get me through my day.

When I first turned Cyrus's head, he claimed my red hair was sexy. But my pregnancy with Lily darkened and thinned it, and the curls he once loved to wrap around his fingers loosened into waves. I swept my long hair back most days, let it towel dry, and then pulled the sides up into bobby pins so that Cyrus wasn't constantly reminded of the way my ginger curls no longer framed my face.

Every morning I dedicated a few minutes to my hair, then applied light makeup and shell-pink lip gloss. I finished my personal routine with dark jeans and an expensive sweater—something fine-woven and cottony during the warm months, and wool or a bulky cable knit when it was cold. Though I shopped in the same stores that his friends' wives frequented, my attire was a source of constant annoyance for Cyrus. It was too modest, too predictable, but it was one area where I didn't give. I wore tops with high collars and sleeves that covered my arms all the way down past my wrists. My fingers peeked out, and my face. That was more than enough of me exposed.

I emerged from the bathroom at exactly six-thirty and went straight to the kitchen to start breakfast. Cyrus didn't have to be at the dealership until eight, but he liked to leave the house by seven. It was common knowledge in Everton that the old boys' club met at the gas station every workday morning for a cup of coffee as they discussed town business and shot the breeze. As the late mayor's son and soon to be new owner of Price Automotive, Cyrus held a place of prestige that was something akin to a throne. He was small-town royalty, one of the richest, most influential men in town, and he wielded his position like a lord. And this particular sovereign liked two eggs for breakfast, over easy, on two slices of white, buttered toast, and a glass of pulp-free orange juice.

Cyrus swept into the kitchen at six-forty-five, just as I was situating the second egg on the second slice of softly browned toast. He sat down at the head of the table in the dining room, gulped the glass of orange juice that was waiting for him, and then dug into the plate that I set before him. Sometimes he acknowledged me. Sometimes not. Sometimes he found fault with his breakfast, or with the day that was breaking outside the picture window at his elbow, or with me. Cyrus didn't usually yell in the morning, but there was always sometimes.

After he left, I threw in a load of laundry, got Lily up, helped her with her before-school routine, and shooed her out the door by eight. Then, when the house was empty and still save for the steady beat of my own muted heart, my day started in earnest. There were rooms to clean and supper to make. There was a long list of boards on which I was expected to volunteer, as well as my women's Bible study and the Rotary Club.

I have to admit, I played the part well. My house was perfectly kept, my kitchen always warm with the fragrance of something freshly baked or a mouthwatering pot roast in the oven. And I had friends at my Bible study, a group of well-kept women just like me, with husbands who were bankers or insurance agents and who accompanied Cyrus on his frequent trips. We shared recipes and parenting tips, and if those ladies with their perma-smiles and French manicures suspected that things were less than storybook between Cyrus and me, they never let on.

When Max called, my perfectly ordered life went up in smoke. I knew my old friend couldn't finish all those custom suits on his own, but I also knew that Cyrus would be furious if he found out what I was doing. And yet, even before Lily convinced me that I really had no choice—I had to help the man who had been surrogate father to me—I was already creating a smokescreen that would, I hoped, hide my subterfuge from Cyrus's prying eyes.

Meetings were rescheduled, absences accounted for with claims of upcoming dentist appointments or haircuts. I resurrected my Crock-Pot cookbook and bought groceries for meals that I could throw together in the slow cooker and then transfer to appropriate pots and pans in the hour before Cyrus came home from work in the evening. And once Lily knew what was going on, she offered to help me keep up with the housework by vacuuming floors or scrubbing bathrooms in stolen moments before and after school.

But even with all my careful planning, my days were so scheduled, so dictated by Cyrus and what he required of me that balancing my life with my short-term work in Max's shop was nearly impossible. And it wasn't long before I started to trip up.

"Dad will be home in fifteen minutes," I told Lily as I pulled an apron over my head. "I'm going to stick the chicken in the oven to brown, and I want you to quick run the vacuum in the living room. It's been a couple of days."

Lily looked like she was about to protest, but my eyes must have held a convincing level of desperation. I considered myself a good secret keeper, but this ruse was already wearing me thin. There was a laundry basket of dirty clothes hidden in one of the spare rooms, and a gray ring developing in the downstairs toilet. I just couldn't keep up with it all.

"Fine," Lily huffed, rolling her eyes.

"Watch the clock," I warned. "Make sure the vacuum is put away by five o'clock at the latest. If Dad closes up on time, he could be home as early as five-oh-two."

"Is there a certain pose you'd like me to strike when he comes through the door?"

My hands stopped in the middle of knotting my apron strings. "Don't be like that," I said. "Please. I need you to help me with this."

"It's been a week, Mom." Lily put her fists on her hips with an authoritative air. She gave me a look that made me wonder if I was the child and she was the adult. "Don't you think it's time to let Dad in on our little secret?"

My heart stopped beating in my chest. "What?" I whispered as it thudded back to life. "No, honey. We can't tell your dad what we're doing."

"But it's Dad," she complained. "He might be mad at first, but he'll understand."

Sometimes I forgot that Lily was just a little girl. A little girl who loved her daddy even though he was distant and uninterested. And though I could congratulate myself for shielding her so well from the dysfunction of our broken family, apparently I had done too good a job of convincing her that everything was just fine. On the outside, we truly are the perfect, All-American family, I thought. We hide our bruises beneath designer sweaters and pretend that Garrison Keillor was right about idyllic small-town life. Maybe I was doing my daughter a disservice by allowing her to believe such falsehoods. But I couldn't bring myself to tell her the truth.

Staring at Lily's sweet, trusting face, I did the only thing I could think of: I stalled. "We'll tell him," I said, hoping God would forgive my small, white lie in light of the giant lie I was living. "But not yet. Okay? I need a bit more time to sort this out. You wouldn't want Dad to forbid us to go to Eden, would you?"

That had the desired effect. Lily already loved Max almost as much as I did, and I knew that she would do anything to preserve our afternoons in his tranquil shop. "No," she said. And then she pretended to lock her lips and throw away the key. It was a reluctant pantomime, but I breathed a sigh of relief all the same. A moment later I heard the sound of the vacuum roaring to life.

After transferring the garlic chicken from the Crock-Pot to a roasting pan, I took a pot of potatoes I had peeled and quartered that morning from the refrigerator and set it to boil on the stove. The table was already set, and I stood in the middle of the kitchen, turning a slow circle and trying to see everything as Cyrus would see it. Did anything look amiss? Was it obvious that I was letting my home life slide?

I was so absorbed in my thoughts that I nearly jumped out of my skin at the staccato of cheerful raps on my front door. Someone was knocking, and it was so unexpected I didn't know what to do for a moment. The Price family didn't get visitors, at least, not unannounced visitors. I swallowed nervously. Had someone seen me sneaking in the back door of Max's shop? Had they come to confront me?

Straightening my apron, I hurried into the entryway of our elegant home. There were no windows in the solid oak door, so I wasn't afforded a sneak peek at my guest. I took a deep breath and fixed a smile on my face. In the moment before I grabbed the handle I caught a glimpse of a telltale silver thread that wound its way around my arm. I plucked it off and let it drift between the leaves of a potted plant in the corner.

My knees were almost shaking by the time I finally opened the door, but the person standing on my front step regarded me with concern, not accusation.

"Sarah," I said, trying to hide my confusion. "What are you doing here?"

The pretty woman before me reached out and put a

hand on my arm. "We missed you at Bible study today," she said.

Sarah Kempers was short and spirited, with a thousand-watt smile that she wasn't afraid to offer lavishly. Some would call her plump, but I thought she was faultlessly proportioned and disarmingly cute—it was next to impossible to be defensive in her presence. It didn't hurt that she was the pastor's wife. The friendly couple practically oozed benevolence.

"Oh," I said distractedly, trying to come up with an excuse that wasn't a blatant lie. "I guess I forgot."

"I called a few times today, but no one answered. I just wanted to make sure everything's okay."

"I was . . . out," I fumbled. "Bible study must have slipped my mind."

She bit her bottom lip for a moment. "It's not like you to forget, Rachel. Are you sure you're all right?"

Sarah seemed genuinely worried, and a faint smile tugged at my mouth in spite of the fear that had gripped me only moments before. "I'm fine," I said. "It means a lot to me that you would stop by."

"It's no bother." She grinned back. "I guess we're just such a tight-knit group that it's painfully obvious when one of us is missing. We missed you today."

Although I was furious with myself for letting something as important as my weekly study slip, it was wonderful to hear that they had missed me. "I'll be there next week," I assured her, and I promised myself that no matter what was happening at Max's shop, I would sneak out for the next Bible study. I couldn't afford to make such a huge blunder again.

"We'll look forward to it," Sarah said. Then, looking past me, her smile seemed to harden a bit. It was an almost imperceptible change, and I wondered if maybe the sun had slanted just so and altered the shadows on her face. But before I could contemplate it further, I heard footsteps on the tile of the entry hall. Lily loved Sarah and I knew she would want to say "hi" if she was done vacuuming.

"Lily, honey, are you done with—?" My breath caught in my throat as Cyrus slid an arm around my waist.

"Done with what?" Cyrus asked, looking down at me. He smelled faintly of exhaust and the overpowering floral air freshener that clung to everything in the dealership offices. In spite of a long day at work, his suit looked clean and starched, and his eyes were bright and curious. "What was Lily doing?"

"Her homework," I said, thankful that the house was silent. She had stopped vacuuming. I just hoped that she had put the appliance away. Cyrus couldn't stand it when things were left lying around the house. "When did you get home?" I asked, hoping that the question sounded light and cheerful. He seemed to be in an unusually good mood, but I knew from personal experience how quickly that could change.

"Just a minute ago. I saw the Kemperses' van parked on the street and thought I'd come say hello."

"Hi, Cyrus," Sarah said. Her voice was perfectly normal, and I decided I must have imagined the sudden steel of her smile.

"Hello, Sarah. What brings you to the Price home today?"

Please don't tell him, I silently begged, terrified that she would explain that I had missed Bible study. I couldn't think of a single plausible excuse, and besides, Cyrus always seemed to know when I was lying. If Sarah said that I was a no-show, it would come out—all of it—and he would force me to stop seeing Max. Though I had spent twelve years without him, now that he was a part of my life again I couldn't imagine losing him. And Max was just a piece of the whole. The freedom, the acceptance that I had known in just one short week of working at Eden Custom Tailoring made me feel like a new person. I couldn't stand the thought of going back to the way things had been.

Sarah's eyes found mine and something unspoken passed between us. It startled me, the brief intensity of her stare, and I held my breath as she turned her attention to my husband.

"Actually, I'm just returning Rachel's book," Sarah said.

I glanced down and found that she was holding out a small, paperback study guide. I hadn't even noticed that she had anything in her hands.

"She forgot it at Bible study this morning."

"She'd forget her head if it wasn't screwed on." Cyrus laughed, taking the book from Sarah. "Thanks for bringing it by. You didn't have to do that."

"I was in the neighborhood," Sarah shrugged. "But, hey, I don't want to interrupt family time. You guys have a great night."

"Thanks, Sarah." There was a bit of a wobble in my voice but I coughed to cover it up. "I mean, really. Thank you."

Sarah turned around at the bottom of the steps and gave me a quick, searching look. Then she laughed her characteristic, sunny laugh and waved good-bye to the two of us standing side by side. We must have cut a strange silhouette hovering just inside the door. I wondered if she could tell how stiff I was, how aware of the heft of Cyrus's body next to mine.

"I'm here for you, Rachel," Sarah said.

Somehow, those five words brimmed with meaning.

CHAPTER 5

RACHEL

October 8

Cyrus closed the front door with a soft click. "Looks like an interesting book," he said, turning the study guide over in his hands. It was one I'd never seen before.

I made a vague, noncommittal noise and tried to calm my racing heart. Being with Cyrus when I couldn't read his mood made me feel like I was surrounded by land mines, and I was so unsettled by my encounter with Sarah that I didn't feel up to the intricate dance required to evade the many pitfalls and traps that marked life with my husband.

His face was a mask of nonchalance, but I didn't know if his deliberate calm was a ruse, or if he truly didn't suspect anything devious in Sarah's appearance on our front step. I hoped more than anything that he wouldn't quiz me about the content of the book. I had no idea what it was or why Sarah had brought it for me.

"Supper will be ready in a minute," I said, trying to direct a smile his way. It came out brittle and uneven. But Cyrus wasn't looking at me anyway; he was flipping through the pages of the book.

" 'There is no fear in love,' " Cyrus read, quoting from the back cover copy. " 'But perfect love casts out fear.' " He snorted. "What are you afraid of, Rachel?"

The question caught me so off-guard I almost answered him. You. But that wasn't entirely true. I was afraid of many things, but nothing so much as the sickening thought that I was the person he said I was. Good-for-nothing. Unloved. I could only imagine the things he would say if he knew that I had been lying to him for the span of an entire week. I stifled a shiver and Cyrus mistook it as evidence of my cowardice.

"Your book is wrong," he said with a smirk. "Love doesn't cast out fear. Power does." Cyrus took a quick step toward me and I flinched. But my apprehension was unwarranted, because all he did was reach around me, his chest pressing against mine in a cheap imitation of the intimacy we knew for such a brief time so many years ago. I held my breath as he yanked open the top drawer of the narrow desk in the hallway. Closed my eyes and willed my hands to stop shaking when I realized what he was doing.

Even though we lived in a small town where crime was virtually nonexistent, Cyrus insisted on keeping a gun in the hall drawer. Just in case, he said, but I had a hard time envisioning any scenario where that gun would be a welcome addition to our home. When Lily was little, he kept the drawer locked with a small silver key that he hid on top of the wide, wooden frame of the hall mirror. But when she turned ten, he showed her the drawer and the gun, and warned her to never, ever touch it unless there was grave danger. Lily was young, but the vein of iron in her daddy's voice ensured that she gave the hall desk a wide berth whenever she had to walk through the entryway. It was a small consolation to me that my daughter seemed more afraid of Cyrus's choice of protection than whatever it was he intended to protect her from.

Now, as my husband lifted the weapon out of the drawer, he did something he had never done before. He took me roughly by the wrist and slapped the gun in my palm. "This should cast out your fear," he said.

The metal was icy cold and much heavier than I had

imagined it would be. Though the gun had collected dust in our entry for over a decade, I had never touched it or even opened the drawer where it lay in wait. "I don't want this!" I gasped, trying to give it back to him.

But Cyrus took a step back, and if I hadn't curled my fingers around the notched grip it would have fallen to the floor.

"What are you doing?" I met my husband's eyes, trying to discern his motives, his strange reasoning for forcing his gun into my hands after all these years. I half expected this to be some sort of test, for Cyrus to be watching my reaction with cool calculation. Surely he knew that I had missed Bible study, and this elaborate masquerade was just a ruse to throw me off-guard. But Cyrus's face wasn't hard. I knew the set of his jaw when he was angry, the way his dark brows knit together in the moment before he exploded. This was different. The half-smile on his face bespoke amusement, not anger.

"I'm going away," he said. "I thought you should know how to use that thing."

"Away?" I parroted lamely.

"Used cars are hot right now," Cyrus said with an easy shrug. "I bought a pair of quality trucks from some guy in California. Jason and I are going to fly into LA and hang out for a while, then drive home when we feel like it."

"You usually hire men to drive for you," I said. Then I shook my head, startled that I dared to question him. I decided I was in a sort of shock. I had expected my husband's fury—not this.

Fortunately, my comment didn't stoke Cyrus's anger. "I feel like doing it myself this time," he said. "I need a vacation."

I gave a meek nod and tried to carefully hand back the gun. But instead of taking it from me, Cyrus merely turned it in my hand.

"The safety is here," he said, flicking a tiny square catch with his fingernail. Then he put his thumb on the hammer and pretended to cock it. "Pull this back, and then all you have to do is point and shoot. An idiot could do it."

Our eyes locked for a second, and I understood that the idiot was me. It was always me. "I don't think I could use it," I said, ducking my head so I didn't have to watch his gaze harden and frost over.

"What if you need to? What if something happens while I'm gone?"

"You've been gone before," I reminded him, studying my feet and saying each word with precise caution. Sometimes I believed that if I moved slowly and spoke softly, I would be able to avoid the tripwires that were scattered all over our seemingly harmless conversations. "I've never needed this."

Cyrus took the gun from me with a derisive grunt. "You've never brought home a book about fear before."

I opened my mouth to say something, but stopped myself before I ruined the tenuous calm. We hadn't fought, not really, and I knew better than to push my luck. Instead, I watched out of the corner of my eye as Cyrus clicked the safety catch a second time and put the gun back in the table drawer. Then he tossed the book beside it and shut the two incongruous items away together. "Worthless waste of paper," he mumbled as he walked away.

I watched his retreat from beneath lowered lashes, and when he disappeared up the stairs to change out of his suit, I whispered the words that I had almost let slip. "You wouldn't understand."

I hadn't even seen the title of the book, but from the passage he had read I knew beyond a shadow of a doubt that the Bible study Sarah had brought me wasn't at all about fear.

It was a book about love.

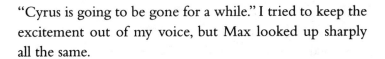

"Cyrus is going to be gone for a while." I tried to keep the excitement out of my voice, but Max looked up sharply all the same.

"Where is he going?"

I feigned nonchalance. "He's picking up some used cars."

"Shouldn't take too long. Here, spread this out for me." Max motioned toward a bolt of jet-black silk that we were transforming into a formal, double-breasted suit coat.

Grabbing the smooth rectangle of cloth, I unwrapped several yards and let it pool on the table.

"It'll just be nice not to have to worry about tiptoeing around the house for a few days."

"You haven't told him about our arrangement yet?"

I snuck a peek at Max and found myself trapped in his knowing gaze. "No," I said, deflating a little. "Of course not. He can't know."

Max opened his mouth. Shut it again. Then he sighed and stood up straight, pressing his fists to the small of his back and rolling out his broad shoulders. "Rachel, Rachel," he murmured. "Will you ever be done?"

He wasn't talking about the suit.

In the week that I had been working with Max, he had never pried into the particulars of my marriage or brought up the strange and heartbreaking edict that Cyrus had passed almost immediately after I said, "I do." It was the elephant in the room, the boulder between us that kept everything sweet and surfacey instead of deep and meaningful like it had been with the Wevers when I was a kid.

I didn't like pretending that nothing was wrong, but in all the years that I had been with Cyrus I had never spoken to anyone about what it was like to be his wife. My secrets were buried deep, and I wasn't sure that I wanted to resurrect them.

And yet, Max's one question was teeming with memories. It unleashed a barrage of dangerous emotions that threw me off guard. Will you ever be done? The first time that Max said a version of those words to me was on my wedding day.

I was eighteen years old when I fell in love with Cyrus, and nineteen when we were married. It was a hasty affair, and people were right when they assumed that it was a shotgun wedding. But there was never any evidence of our indiscretion—I lost our first baby to miscarriage only a few weeks after Cyrus and I said our vows. Sometimes I couldn't help but wonder if things would have been different if that baby we never knew had never been. Would I have married Cyrus? Or would I have listened to Max and run as fast and as far as I could?

Max and Elena tried to talk me out of marrying Cyrus up until the last possible moment. At first my surrogate father had even refused to walk me down the aisle, saying that my real dad deserved the honor. But my dad hated Cyrus, and the feeling was more than mutual. I knew that I could have one or the other—my dad or the love of my life—not both. I had already made my decision, and I would have given myself away to Cyrus if that's what it came down to. In the end, Max relented, but standing in the back of the church as we watched the bridesmaids disappear one by one, he made one last-ditch effort to convince me that I was making the biggest mistake of my life.

"He's controlling," Max whispered. His voice was tense and urgent.

"Cyrus's not controlling," I said, patting Max on the arm. We were linked at the elbows, our heads bent together as if we were having a final, tender moment on the most momentous day of my life. Anyone who saw us would think we were sharing a dream for my future. "He's protective."

"He's manipulative." Max all but growled.

"He wants what's best for me."

"He's dangerous."

I laughed a little at that. Cyrus wasn't dangerous. He was exciting and passionate and the perfect amount of wild. There was something brooding and untamed just below the surface, but I loved that side of him. He made me feel intoxicated. Alive.

It seemed that Max could read my mind. He squeezed my hand. "Rachel, honey, I don't trust him."

"I trust him with my life." The words rolled off my tongue, but even as I said them I wondered if they were true. I was certainly attracted to Cyrus, and we loved each other enough to make a baby, but there was only one man I trusted with my life and he was standing beside me. But I couldn't say any of that. Not when the string quartet began to play the Wedding March and the congregation rose to their feet for my entrance.

I took a deep breath and snuck a peek at Max. He was devouring me with his eyes, his expression pained and desperate. I saw the storm that raged inside him, but just when I feared he was going to whisk me out of the church and away from the man I was about to marry, he pulled me into a rough embrace. "You let me know when you're done," he whispered into my hair.

It was a bewildering statement, but I didn't have time to ponder it. The doors to the sanctuary opened for us, and Max and I began our slow march down the aisle.

The processional seemed to take a lifetime, and the closer I got to Cyrus the farther away I felt from everything I knew. I wasn't regretting my decision as much as I was stunned that I had chosen to ignore Max and Elena—and my father—when they tried to share their reservations about Cyrus Price. What if they were right? What if instead of wedded bliss my future only held a time when this would all be over? When I would be done?

It couldn't be. Everyone else had to be wrong. I didn't deserve Cyrus, he was too good for a blue-collar girl like me. A girl who came from such brokenness. And still, there he stood at the front of the church, watching me come with a lopsided, knowing smirk. I blushed at the fire in his eyes, the surfer-boy sweep of his sandy hair, and the sharp line of his angled jaw. He was beautiful, and he was mine.

By the time Max and I reached the end of the long aisle, I was nearly bursting with anticipation. Marrying Cyrus was my own fairytale come true, and Max's words were all but forgotten when my groom reached for my hand. But before Max let me go, he leaned toward Cyrus and gave him a sort of one-armed embrace. The three of us were pulled into a huddle, a place where the only thing we could hear was the sound of our own breathing. I'm sure it was a touching sight for all of our family and friends gathered in the pews.

It wasn't touching from where I stood. Max glared at Cyrus and Cyrus glared back. Then my gray-haired defender gave my soon-to-be husband a crisp smile and said, "I'm watching you."

In the circle of their arms, there was a split second of hushed silence. Less than a heartbeat of stillness during which Cyrus's eyes flinted with something that looked very much like fear. I could almost imagine him as a little boy, caught redhanded in the act of doing something deplorable. And Max had his number. But just as quickly as the expression flared, it dulled. Cyrus licked his lips as if he longed to spit at Max's feet, but instead he turned to me. He gave me a brilliant, heart-stopping smile and pulled me toward him. My fingers slipped from Max's arm, and just like that my fate was sealed.

The rest of the ceremony was a blur, but I'll never forget what Cyrus said the moment we burst through the back doors of the church. Birdseed anointed our heads and the train of my hand-stitched dress was thrown over my arm so that I could run down the steps and into my new life. I was so caught up in the music and the tears, the vows we had shared, that I had all but forgotten Max and what he had said. But Cyrus hadn't. My toe hadn't yet graced the first stair when Cyrus put his mouth to my ear and whispered viciously, "You will never speak to that man again. Ever."

Never. The word cut like a knife, slicing away what had been and what would be. Separating me from the closest thing I had to a father. Cyrus had already put the final nail in the coffin of my relationship with my dad. Now this?

In the beginning I thought that Cyrus would soften. That there would come a day when he would realize that he had been overreacting, and that Max and Elena meant the world to me. But he didn't back down. Even when I lost the baby and couldn't stop crying for days, he refused to let me see the couple that I considered my family.

So I lied. I snuck out to see them, and when Cyrus found out he hit me.

It was the first time he ever raised a hand against me, and though the unanticipated blow lashed straight through my wounded heart, I understood why he did it. I had defied him, hadn't I? I had done the one thing he asked me not to do.

It was a slap. Nothing, really.

Maybe Max thought I would run then. Maybe he thought I would be done. But I had been hurt before. I think Max underestimated my ability to pick myself up and keep going. Done? Far from it.

But now, over a decade later, to hear my surrogate father say those words stirred something savage inside me. I didn't even know that I could feel that way, that I could be filled with a longing so raw and unexpected that it brought tears to my eyes. Bowing my head over the sewing table, I took a shuddering breath.

"I know who he is," Max said softly. "I see what he does. Please, Rachel. You don't have to live like this. You know that, don't you?"

I shook my head as if to clear it. "I have a daughter now," I said. "Lily needs her dad."

"Not like this." Max moved around the table and reached a hand out for me. His fingers brushed the fabric of my sweater for just a moment before he seemed to accept that

I wouldn't respond to his touch. That I was unreachable. He changed tactics. "He still hits you, doesn't he?"

"Not really," I said. "Not often."

"Rachel, abuse is abuse—"

"I am not an abused woman." My voice was flinty, furious. "Don't you dare make me out to be some weakling."

"I don't think you're weak. I think you're strong," Max said. "But it kills me to see you like this. And I can't stand the thought that he dares to raise a hand against you."

All the fight went out of me in one long exhalation. "He's just a big bully, Max. He likes to get his way and when things don't go as planned he overreacts. I know how to deal with him. Besides, what would you have me do? Leave?"

"Exactly."

I shook my head at that. "Where would I go? What would I do? I have a high school education and zero credentials. Everything and everyone I know is here. I'm not going anywhere. I can't."

"But you could—"

The sound of Lily's backpack hitting the floor behind us cut Max off so quickly he seemed to inhale whatever it was he was about to say. We both spun around, shocked that we had let the time get away from us, and downright sickened to realize that even if she hadn't heard our entire conversation, Lily had heard enough of it.

"Lil, honey," I said, taking a tentative step toward her. "How long have you been standing there?"

Her face was stricken, her mouth a thin, serious line. She stumbled backward a bit and bumped into the doorframe.

"Listen to me, Lily. You overheard a conversation that wasn't meant for your ears. I know you don't understand, but you have to believe me—"

"Believe you?" Lily's eyes went wide. "Believe you? You're a liar!" She whipped around and flew out the back room of the bridal shop, letting the steel door slam behind her.

CHAPTER 6

MITCH

December 24, 10:00 A.M.

The atrium is warm and bright, filled with the contented hum of activity. There is a TV on in the corner, and there are little knots of people congregating around tables and in carefully arranged nooks. Mitch's eyes flick past the shuffleboard table and pause for a moment on the aviary that takes up the entire south wall. It's impossible not to admire the tiny birds and the way they make the air seem to shimmer with their songs. But though the birds are lovely, Mitch would rather watch the residents.

Three of the elderly inhabitants of The Heritage

Home are with their visiting families. One gentleman—the one closest to where Mitch stands—is smiling as he unwraps a Christmas present. It's a misshapen clay bowl, the sort of handmade work of art that is worth far more than diamonds or pearls. The little girl who made it grins as she points out its various attributes, and when her grandfather tells her that her gift is beautiful, just what he wanted, she throws her arms around his neck. Whispers loud enough for Mitch to hear, "I love you."

Those words stab through Mitch and leave him breathless. How long has it been since he's made so bold, so life-changing a declaration? Since he's heard it? He can't remember.

"I brought the chess board in case you're up for it."

Mitch turns to find a well-dressed man at his elbow. He can feel his brow furrow in confusion, but before he can formulate a polite question the man smiles.

"Cooper," he says. "We were going to play a game."

"I don't know how to play chess." Mitch gives the perplexing bag of stone pieces a furtive glance. For some reason he knows that the carved tokens are pawns and knights, rooks and royalty. But he can't imagine what they are supposed to do.

"Good thing I brought the checkers, too." Cooper spins his hand and reveals a second cloth bag. This one is filled with red and black disks.

"I don't think I know how to play checkers either."

"It's easy. I can teach you in less than five minutes. You'll probably mop the floor up with me."

Mitch lets himself be led to a small table near a span of floor-to-ceiling windows. The day is soft and gray, muted with the silence of a storybook snowfall. It is a lovely sight, but one look at the gentle storm and Mitch knows that the roads will be a nightmare in no time at all. The plows simply won't be able to keep up with the volume.

"I drove a plow," Mitch says, staring out the window.

"You had a plow attached to the front of your work truck," Cooper amends. He lays out the checkered board between them and begins to methodically place the red playing pieces on the black squares in front of him. "You could bolt the plow blade on in the winter, and take it off in the summer. It was a side job."

"A side job?"

"A way to make some extra cash. Construction slows down a lot in the winter, you know."

Construction. Mitch looks at his hands and is warmed by the certainty that he was good at what he did. The corner of his mouth tweaks as his body remembers what it was like to jump from one roof truss to the next. He had amazing balance. He could walk from one side of an unfinished building to the other, skimming the narrow boards with his feet and never once catching anything for support. A part of him would like to tell Cooper this, but the stranger beats him to the punch.

"You should have been an architect," he says. "You had an eye for it. It takes someone special to build a home, and you built the best."

The rush of pride that Mitch feels is short-lived as understanding spills over him. "A home is more than a building," he says. It seems like a profound thought. Something he should have realized sooner.

Cooper looks up and meets his gaze. "You're right. A home is much more than a building." He seems to want Mitch to say something, but for the life of him Mitch can't figure out what it might be.

Instead of responding, Mitch reaches for the checkers and begins to copy the pattern that Cooper made. Black tiles on black spaces.

When they start to play, the rules come back to Mitch like riding a bike. He jumps three of Cooper's checkers and soon has control over the board. The game doesn't require much thought, but when Mitch reaches for the bag of chess pieces and fingers the individual tiles, he's disappointed to find that they are still meaningless bits of stone to him. He simply doesn't feel up to trying.

"You seem sad today," Cooper comments when Mitch deposits the bag back on the table between them.

It's a rather forward thing to say, but Cooper seems to think that they're on pretty familiar terms. Mitch decides not to be cranky because he doesn't want to offend the only person in the entire atrium who has paid him an ounce of attention. "I have a hard time remembering some things," he admits.

"Don't we all." Cooper slides a checker into an unprotected corner of the board. "King me."

Mitch obliges, crowning Cooper's red disk with an extra from the pile he's amassed. "This feels different," Mitch says. "It's a different kind of forgetful."

"It's Alzheimer's." Cooper's proclamation is matter-of-fact.

"Is it bad?"

"Bad enough."

Mitch considers this for a moment. "My memory feels like Swiss cheese. Full of holes."

Cooper laughs. "I like that. Swiss cheese."

"I can almost taste it," Mitch says. "Swiss cheese, I mean. Why can I remember the taste of cheese, but I can't remember how to play chess?"

"You were never a very good chess player."

"I wasn't?"

"Nah." Cooper gives Mitch a serious look. "You only started playing because your daughter joined the chess club in high school. You wanted to be able to play with her. Do you remember that?"

Mitch holds his breath, trying to conjure up the image of playing chess with his teenage daughter. How tall was she? Did she have dark hair or light? Blue eyes or brown? Green? It breaks his heart that he can't picture her, but just as he is about to give up he feels a flicker of her at the very edge of his memory.

She's a wisp of a thing, slight and lovely with big, haunted eyes. Mitch is leveled by a yearning to pull her out of the past and hold her, she looks so life-weary and broken. But as much as he wants to hug her now, he can't fight the sudden knowledge that he didn't often hold her when he had the chance.

"I was a bad father," Mitch says, his voice cracking.

Cooper shakes his head. "You weren't a bad father."

"I didn't know how to be a father. Especially the father of a daughter. What did I know about little girls?"

"Well, it's not like children come with instruction manuals. You did the best you could."

"I don't think my best was good enough." Mitch battles the quick and furious desire to fling the chessboard off the table. To shout. To break something. But what would that accomplish? He knows that things were thrown in his home, and that they had no peace to show for it. All the fight fizzles out of him. "She was sad, wasn't she?"

"That wasn't your fault," Cooper says, but it's little consolation. "Life is sad sometimes."

"My wife . . ." Mitch trails off, afraid to finish the sentence. "My wife said things, and she did things . . ."

"See?" Cooper sweeps his hands as if Mitch's unfinished thought excuses everything. "Your wife did things. Not you."

"Does it matter who did what?" Mitch may not remember his address or what his teenage daughter looked like, but he does know that there are sins of omission as surely as there are sins of commission. Whether or not he did anything, he carries the guilt of turning a blind eye. It's devastating. He can't stand the man that he thinks he was, and he can't recognize the man that he is. The past is a blur of emotion and fragments of memories that make him feel dizzy and bewildered. He wants nothing more than to be able to lay the years out before him—ugliness and all—and see his life for what it really was. He can't shake the feeling that it was one colossal failure.

"I can see her, Cooper." Mitch takes his head in his hands and tries to make the flicker of a girl in his mind's eye stay put. "I can see her but I can't touch her. I can't say the things that I want to say to her."

Cooper's silence stretches on so long that Mitch finally looks up. The man across from him is wearing an expression that is rife with pity. With compassion. "What would you say to her if you could?"

Mitch doesn't pause for a second. "I'd tell her that I'm sorry. That I should have protected her." He squeezes his eyes shut and makes a wish on every single flake of falling snow. "I'd tell her that I love her."

CHAPTER 7

RACHEL

October 8

I found Lily in the center of her four-poster bed with the white lace curtains drawn. Her knees were pulled up to her chest and her eyes were squeezed shut, but even from behind the veil of translucent fabric I could see that she wasn't asleep. My Sleeping Beauty who was too heartbroken to slumber.

"Is this seat taken?" It was a lame attempt at humor, and Lily didn't respond. Instead of waiting for an invitation, I pushed aside the sheer screen and perched on the edge of her bed. "I know you're not sleeping, honey."

"Yes, I am." Lily rolled over, giving me her back. She was curled in a tight ball, her knees pulled up to her chest and a teddy bear tucked amid the tangle of her slender limbs. "Go away," she added, almost as an afterthought.

"I'm not going anywhere," I whispered. Maybe it was the wrong thing to say, but I believed at that moment that what she needed to hear more than anything was that I would stay. "I'm here for you, Lil. I always will be."

We stayed like that for a long time. I smoothed her lavender duvet with my fingers, and Lily breathed in and out, trying to ignore me. She was wrapped around herself, hemming me out as if she was the only person in the world she could trust. I could hardly blame her. I hadn't exactly been honest with her throughout her eleven years of life. Perhaps I was wrong for thinking that some things are better left unsaid.

"I was only trying to protect you." I spoke quietly. "I know what it's like to be alone, to feel like no one will stand between you and the monster under your bed."

"There's no monster under my bed." Lily's voice was muffled by the fur of her teddy bear.

I gave a hollow laugh. "There was no monster under my bed either. It's an expression."

"I know." Lily went perfectly still for a moment, I could tell she was holding her breath, trying to decide if she could say the words that crowded her mouth. After a long moment, she dared. "Is Dad the monster?"

It was an impossible question. Yes. And no. "Dad has a funny way of dealing with life, Lil. That doesn't make him a monster, but sometimes he does some pretty monstrous things."

"I hate him."

The ferocity of her declaration shocked me. Lily had never shown anything more than polite detachment toward her father. Cyrus hadn't been very involved in her younger years, and when her attempts at a relationship were steadily rebuffed as she got older, Lily learned to exist in a home where the man she called her dad was little more than a prop. He brought home the paycheck and sat across from her at the dinner table every night, but he didn't take much interest in her and she learned to mimic his behavior. Lily was no daddy's girl, but she had no reason to hate him either.

"You do not," I said.

"I do!" Lily pushed herself up and whirled to face me. "He hurt you! How could he ... how could anyone...?"

"It's not as simple as it sounds." I put a pacifying hand on her arm and gave her a gentle squeeze. "I've made a lot of mistakes, too. And I'm not the same woman that he married all those years ago."

"What do you mean?" Lily passed a hand over her cheeks, swiping at imaginary tears even though her eyes were dry.

I smiled wryly. "You might not believe this, but your mom was once passably pretty."

Lily's mouth dropped open a bit. "What are you talking about? Mom, you're gorgeous. All my friends think so. Amber's mom even told me that Dad married you because you were the best-looking woman this side of the Mississippi."

"Were. I'm an old lady, Lil."

"Give me a break. You're thirty-one." Lily looked me in the eyes, her gaze earnest, insistent. "You really are beautiful, Mom. If Dad doesn't think so, he's blind."

"That's nice of you to say," I murmured, patting her arm absently.

"You don't believe me, do you?" Lily looked confused. "You really don't believe me. How can you not see yourself the way everyone else sees you?"

"Enough." I didn't mean to sound harsh, but my daughter shrank back a bit anyway. "This is silly."

"But I just want you to know that—"

"Lily, stop." I took a deep breath. "It doesn't matter what I look like, honey. What matters is you. All I want—all I've ever wanted—is for you to be happy. I've tried to shield you from . . ." I fumbled for the right words, my hands

fluffing the air as if to encompass the whole of our fabri-
cated lives. "From this."

Lily pressed her teddy bear to her chest hard enough to
make his fat arms look like sausages. She watched me for
a long minute, and I could see the thoughts spin behind
her clear eyes. Finally she seemed to reach a conclusion.
Carefully setting the bear aside, she held out her hands to
me. "You should have told me," she said when I wove my
fingers through hers. "I can take it."

"But—"

"I want to know the truth," Lily said.

"You don't know what you're asking for."

"I do." Lily narrowed her eyes. "I might be a kid, but
I'm not stupid." She slid her hand up my arm and pushed
the sleeve of my sweater away from my wrist. There were
three yellow marks there, all that remained of an old bruise.
Cyrus had just grabbed me harder than he meant to, but
the end result was the same: I had evidence to cover.

"It's nothing," I said, tugging the sleeve back down.

"Fine." Lily threw herself back on the bed and pulled
the covers up to her chin. "Go away, Mom. I want to be
alone."

I knew in that moment that I stood at a crossroads. I
could go on pretending that everything was okay; I could
continue to whitewash a home that was slowly, endlessly de-
caying. Or I could admit that the facade was only as deep as

the thinnest coat of smiles and lies. As I studied my daughter's huddled form, I realized that maintaining the deception was no life at all. Lily would never trust me again if I wasn't honest with her. And I couldn't lose my baby.

"What do you want to know?" I breathed the question so softly I wondered if she would even hear me.

"Everything," Lily said definitively.

I squeezed my eyes shut and wished her request away. But I knew that she wouldn't back down. My daughter was strong in ways I could only imagine. "Okay," I said after several long heartbeats. "It's not a pretty story."

"I don't care."

"I'm not a storyteller."

"Mom." Lily rolled to face me. "Stop making excuses. I want to know."

"Why?"

She bit her bottom lip, considering. Then she sighed a little. "Because no one stood between you and the monster under your bed."

My throat tightened. "Sweetheart . . ."

"I know it's probably too late," Lily continued, "but you once told me that sometimes all you need is someone to listen." She gave me a brave, beautiful smile. "I'm listening."

When I was Lily's age, I knew beyond a shadow of a doubt that no one was listening. I had already taken to calling my mother Bev, not because she asked me to, but because she didn't seem like much of a mom to me. My friends had mothers who baked cookies for them and braided their hair. My so-called mom told me cookies would make me fat and assured me that no amount of braiding would tame my curls. Her verbal abuse was hurtful in the beginning, but by the time I was old enough to realize what she was doing, it didn't pain me so much anymore. Instead, I avoided her as much as possible and shrank away from the rest of the world for good measure.

Bev called me "mousy" once—a rather mild put-down in light of her usual slander—and after I met a mouse up close and personal I decided that I rather liked the comparison. I would happily be mousy all the days of my life.

One of the boys in my fifth-grade class caught a baby field mouse in his backyard and brought it in to our science class for show and tell. The little mouse became a mascot of sorts, and our teacher allowed us to keep it in an old aquarium that we filled with wood shavings and some old hamster paraphernalia that someone donated. Everyone loved the mouse, but no one understood the tiny brown-and-white pup quite like I did.

I loved to watch her curl into a perfect ball, her body round and seamless as a chestnut. She blended into the

wood chips, so still and so perfectly camouflaged as to
be invisible. And when the tiny mouse emerged to eat or
drink, it was when no one else was looking. She seemed
to tiptoe across the aquarium, sneaking furtive glances
left and right and spinning herself into an impenetrable
knot if anyone dared to knock on the glass. Her ability
to blend in was admirable, and when the rest of my classmates lost interest in her I considered it a mouse-sized vic-
tory. She was autonomous, untouchable. I tried to be the
same.

Of course, it didn't work very well. Bev needed someone to be angry at, and whether I wanted to admit it or
not, I still needed a parent in my life. My dad was always
working, working, working, so when I required the assistance of an adult, it usually fell to my alcoholic mother.
Besides, I remembered all too well the sort of help my dad
could offer. The hideous Easter dress I wore went down in
infamy among my peers.

If the dress incident with my dad was his personal low
point, the worst memory I had of Bev was a snapshot
taken at the junior high bake sale. We were trying to raise
money for new band instruments, and everyone had to
contribute in some way. As I reached my hand into the ice
cream bucket filled with scraps of paper that outlined our
various tasks, I prayed that I would emerge with one of
the duties that I could perform alone: painting signs, tak-

ing money, or cleaning up after the event. Instead, I picked baking. I had to bake four dozen cookies to sell.

I didn't know the first thing about baking, and I was pretty sure that Bev didn't either. But I found a recipe on the back of a bag of stale chocolate chips in our pantry, and decided that one way or another I would struggle my way through. It seemed easy enough. The ingredients were listed in order, and the instructions were very straightforward.

There was a large glass bowl in the corner cupboard that I assumed would be big enough to hold the dough. At least, it looked about the right size if I could trust the Toll House commercials. I set the bowl in the middle of the counter, and then collected everything I could find from the pantry and refrigerator. The only ingredient that gave me trouble was baking soda. I couldn't find anything called baking soda, but there was a tall, narrow cylinder that had Clabber Girl Baking Powder on the label. I figured that was close enough.

It only took me half an hour to assemble everything in the order given. My biggest hang-up was sifting the dry ingredients. I didn't know what it meant to sift, so I had to halt the entire process and look it up in the dictionary. To separate something. To put through a sieve; to remove large particles. We didn't have a sieve; at least, I didn't think we did. So I used a slotted spoon to sift the flour, baking powder, and salt to the best of my ability. It worked okay. It wasn't as disastrous as my attempt at cracking eggs.

I was pretty proud of myself by the time the first batch of cookies was in the oven. It felt like a huge accomplishment, knowing that I could not only make something from scratch, but do it entirely on my own. I even imagined telling everyone at the bake sale that the secret baker behind the delicious chocolate chip cookies was none other than mousy old me.

It didn't take long for the warm, inviting smell of baking cookies to draw Bev to the kitchen. Since it was late in the afternoon, she had to hang on to the doorframe to stop herself from tipping over. I remember being mildly surprised that she hadn't stirred amid all the ruckus and noise of my first attempt at baking, but the subtle scent of cookies roused her from wherever she had escaped to.

"What are you making?" Bev had a habit of overenunciating her words when she was tipsy. But her tongue was thick and swollen, and they never came out quite right. She sounded like a speech coach with a wad of cotton in her mouth.

"Cookies. The junior high bake sale is tomorrow."

"I didn't know you could bake."

"Neither did I." I was prepared for a verbal onslaught, but Bev seemed too surprised at my newfound talent to muster an appropriately nasty comeback. Instead, she walked carefully to the table and sat down heavily on one of the chairs. "I need four dozen for school," I warned her. "I don't know if I'll have any leftovers."

"You will."

I couldn't figure out how to work the timer on the stove, so I watched the clock like a hawk for the entire ten minutes of baking time. When it was finally up, I opened the oven door with serious trepidation, and was rewarded by the sight of perfect, round cookies dented with hot pools of melted chocolate chips. To say I was elated would be an understatement, and I think the fierce joy I felt in that moment only made it that much worse when Bev bit into my first cookie and spat it right back out.

"What did you put into these things?" She demanded.

My heart sank. "What do you mean? I followed the instructions . . ."

Bev pushed herself up from the table and began to paw through the ingredients that still littered the counter. She passed right over the demolished egg shells and the little bottle of imitation vanilla I had found in the cupboard. Her hand finally stopped on the cylinder of baking powder. I watched as she looked at it for a moment, a wrinkle of confusion parting her brow. Then she snorted a giggle. "Baking powder? You put baking powder in the cookies? I don't know much about cooking, but I do know you can't use baking powder in place of baking soda!"

"I didn't know," I stuttered as she began to laugh. Maybe she was playing a joke on me. The cookies looked fine. They smelled fine. I grabbed one and took a bite.

Bitter. They were salty and bitter and starting to flatten.

"I didn't know," I repeated, feeling the tears begin to form in my eyes.

If Bev noticed how upset I was, it didn't seem to faze her. "That's why they print instructions," she snorted, leaving the room with a decidedly careful gait: heel, toe, heel, toe. "The ability to read is a prerequisite of baking."

My mother had laughed at me before, but the hot shame of what I thought would be my glory was one of the deepest wounds Bev ever inflicted on me. I cleaned up the kitchen with shaking hands, and when I spilled flour on the floor I had to get down on my hands and knees and scrub it like a chambermaid. In that moment, with the cold linoleum bruising my shins and the seemingly perfect cookie dough discarded in one lumpy mass in the garbage can, I vowed that I would never make such a fool of myself again. Before I left the kitchen, I grabbed Bev's small library of cookbooks and began the slow process of reading each one cover to cover. The next time I made cookies, they were bakery perfect.

But my second attempt at baking didn't happen for another six weeks, and in the meantime I was still required to produce four dozen goodies for the junior high bake sale.

I only had one option. When my dad came home from work that night, I sidled up to his La-Z-Boy and made my plea. His hair was still wet from the shower and exhaustion radiated off him like cheap cologne. I thought he was watching TV, but a second glance revealed that he had fallen asleep with the remote in his hand. Again. I didn't want to disturb him, but I figured I didn't really have a choice.

"Dad?"

He didn't respond.

"Dad?" I gave his shoulder a little shake.

"Wha-what?" He startled awake, straining the springs in his life-beaten chair. "Oh, Rachel, you scared me half to death. Was I sleeping?"

Of course, you were sleeping, I wanted to say. You work and sleep. What else is there? But I didn't say that. I just gave him a little nod and launched into my rehearsed speech. I explained the bake sale and skimmed over my culinary failure, highlighting the fact that Bev was not exactly Betty Crocker. I couldn't count on her to provide something for me.

"You want me to bake something?" Dad asked. The fact that his eyes were round as my ruined cookies assured me that he boasted no hidden talent with a spatula.

"I guess not," I murmured. My shoulders slumped and I turned away without another word. I would bring nothing, and suffer the derision of my classmates and teachers. There was no other option.

But the chair squeaked behind me, and before I could slink away to my room, Dad caught me by the arm. "Hey," he said. "I can't bake, but we can buy something."

"We're supposed to do it ourselves."

"Semantics," he smiled. "We'll buy it ourselves."

"Everyone will know my goodies aren't homemade."

"Not if we buy them from the bakery."

"That's too obvious," I pointed out. "Everyone knows what the bakery cookies look like and taste like."

"We'll rough them up somehow." Dad narrowed his eyes as he thought. "I know! We'll buy plain sugar cookies and then frost them and put sprinkles on top. No one will be able to tell that they're store-bought cookies. At least, not by looking at them."

As I considered the possibility, a ghost of a smile passed over my lips. All my cookies had to do was fool my classmates. I didn't care if whoever bought them later suspected that they came from the Everton bakery. "Okay." I shrugged.

"Okay?"

"It might work."

"It'll definitely work." Dad actually seemed excited by the possibility. "I'll go get what we need while you finish your homework. We can have everything done by bedtime and no one will ever be the wiser. Our secret."

My smile was tightlipped, cautious.

"Come on," he coaxed, holding out his pinky to seal the deal. I was too old for such gestures, but he looked so happy and earnest that after a moment I linked my pinky with his. We shook.

For half an hour while he was gone, I felt an almost unnatural peace. My cookies might have been a flop, but my dad had actually come to the rescue. And even though I would normally be skeptical about such a harebrained idea, it sounded to me like it just might work.

I rode a wave of optimism until Dad came back from the store with a plastic grocery bag in his hand instead of a white box with the Everton bakery stamp.

"I thought you were going to the bakery," I said, confused.

Dad didn't bother taking off his coat. He crossed the kitchen in a few strides and sat beside me at the table. "We weren't thinking, Rach. The bakery is closed."

I deflated so quickly it was as if his words were needles. Of course the bakery was closed. It was eight o'clock on a Tuesday night. It had been closed for hours. "What's in the bag?" I muttered.

Instead of answering, Dad drew out a package of Chips

Ahoy cookies. "It's the best I could do," he said. His eyes pleaded with me to understand. "I looked everywhere. But you know how small the grocery store is. They don't stock many baked goods, and at this time of night the shelves were empty . . ." He was rambling, but the sting of disappointment was too sharp, too fresh for me to give him any sort of reprieve. "It was either this or Oreos, Rach. Look, I bought some frosting, too, and we can still doctor these up. We could make little sandwiches out of them or something . . ."

"No thanks." I pushed away from the table. "I won't take anything."

"But—"

"I said, no thanks." Maybe I should have lessened the sting a little. Maybe I should have said, It was a good idea. But I didn't have the heart. The truth was, a good intention was nothing more than a hollow promise. And I knew all about that particular emptiness.

CHAPTER 8

RACHEL

October 15

With Cyrus gone to the West Coast, I didn't need to worry about keeping my weekly engagements. I could even skip Bible study. But after Sarah covered for me, I almost craved her company. I felt like we had a connection, and even though I wasn't willing to share my secrets with her, a small part of me wanted to. I trusted her. Or I was beginning to trust her.

The coffee shop where we met once a week was warm and smelled of cider and freshly baked bread. A quick scan of the room revealed that the ladies in my Bible study had already claimed a table in the back corner. I slipped off my sunglasses and began to make my way across the tile floor. But before I reached our designated study spot, Sarah stood up and came to greet me.

"Sorry, I'm late," I said, silently cursing myself for staying an extra minute with Max. We were right in the middle of something, but I should have dropped it all the same. I didn't want to arouse any more suspicion.

"Oh, you're not late." Sarah smiled. "I just wanted to catch you before we enter the melee." She snagged a thumb over her shoulder at the exact moment the women at the table burst out laughing. We took our Bible study seriously, but no one could deny that we were a fun group of girls. Or, at least, the rest of them were fun. I usually buried my laughter deep and considered myself lucky that they made room for me in spite of my reputation for solemnity.

"Is something wrong?" I asked, trying to keep my voice light.

"Not at all." Sarah took me by the arm and steered me toward the counter where a spiky-haired barista waited to take our orders. "Coffee's on me this morning. A skinny hazelnut latte? Tall?"

I nodded.

"Make it two." Sarah directed her last comment at the barista, and began fishing around in her purse for her wallet. A moment later the espresso machine whirred to life and we were enveloped by the familiar din of Everton's only coffee shop. Sarah used the blanket of noise to lean close to me. "I hope I didn't get you in trouble last week."

I knew exactly what she was talking about, but her choice of words threw me off guard. Trouble? Was it that obvious that Cyrus ran a tight ship? I shook my head. "Not at all. Thanks for covering for me."

"It's kind of disturbing how easily the lie fell off my tongue." Sarah's eyes sparkled. She didn't seem the least bit upset that she had been less than honest with my husband.

"I thought lying was a sin," I said, not even sure myself if I was teasing or baiting her.

Sarah's expression went flat. "So is hurting your wife."

Her words were a sucker punch to the gut. I almost bent in half. "What?"

"Thought so." Sarah softened immediately and tucked her bottom lip between her teeth in an expression that was a mixture of compassion and contrition. "I'm sorry, Rachel, I didn't mean to spring that on you. It's just, I've suspected for a really long time."

"And now you know," I whispered. There was venom in my voice.

"No!" Sarah fell back a little. "No, you don't understand—"

"I suppose I can expect your husband to make a house

call," I said through gritted teeth. "Maybe he'll suggest some couple's counseling. Or maybe I'm not praying hard enough."

"That's not it at all . . ." Sarah looked genuinely devastated, but I was too incensed to care.

"It's none of your business," I said.

"Rachel," Sarah's voice broke, "I really am sorry. I'm just trying to be your friend. I didn't mean to—"

But I never got to hear what Sarah didn't mean, because at that exact moment the coffee machine screeched to a stop and we were bathed in an almost eerie silence. We stood there for a few seconds, just staring at each other, and then I hiked up my purse on my shoulder and turned to go.

"I just remembered something I have to do," I said.

"Please don't go," Sarah said quietly. I could almost hear her fumbling for something more to say. "Your coffee . . ."

"You drink it," I said. "I'm not thirsty."

When I told Max what had happened at the coffee shop, he was less than sympathetic. "Sounds to me like she's just trying to look out for you."

"She's prying!" I spat. "It's none of her business."

"It is if she's your friend. Is she your friend?"

I had to think about that. Keeping friends had never been my strong suit, but if anyone was a friend to me, it was definitely Sarah. We had been in the same Bible study for four years straight, and she had shown me nothing but kindness. Of course, we weren't the sort to spend time at each other's houses, and we never got together with our families, but then, I couldn't exactly parade my marriage around like that. Cyrus and I usually went our separate ways, and when my presence was required at a social function I played the part of his demure escort admirably. I knew my place. But none of that negated the fact that Sarah made me smile. That I looked forward to seeing her, and that she knew more about me than most of the people in my hometown.

"Yes," I finally said with a hint of resignation. "Sarah is a friend."

"Then it's her responsibility to look after you. It's in the fine print: Friends should always protect, always trust, always hope, always persevere." Max smoothed a chocolate-colored tweed and began the slow process of pinning the jacket pattern to the fabric.

I pursed my lips. "You've got the quote wrong. I believe it begins with: 'Love is patient, love is kind . . . Love should always protect.' "

"Sure it does. But I didn't get the passage wrong. Sarah is trying to be a friend—she's trying to love you."

"She ambushed me," I muttered. And yet, my anger was slipping through my fingers. How could I be upset when my chest was filled with warmth at the unexpected thought that Sarah might not only consider me a friend, she might actually love me?

"I'll agree that her technique could use some work, but it's obvious she cares a lot about you. She brought you the book, she covered for you with Cyrus, and now she's trying to reach out to you." Max refused to meet my gaze, but I could tell that he was very pleased with Sarah's tenacity. "You've got yourself a good friend there."

I exhaled slowly. "I had myself a good friend."

"What's that supposed to mean?"

"I basically yelled at her in front of a dozen people. I can't imagine she took that very well."

Max laughed. "Sweetie, we didn't talk for twelve years. Twelve years. And Elena and I never stopped loving you for even a second of it. A true friendship can withstand a lot. From what I've heard, I believe that Sarah is a true friend."

"Sarah Kempers?" Lily asked, coming through the door to the back room. She was wearing a green turtleneck sweater that set off her eyes, and her strawberry hair hung in wind-tousled ringlets around her flushed cheeks. I couldn't help but marvel at her as she came around the table and gave Max a one-armed hug. She turned back to me. "You mean the pastor's wife, right? I like her."

"I do, too," I sighed. "I just hope I haven't scared her away."

"How did you scare her away?"

"It's a long story," I said, giving my attention to the work before me. "How was school today?"

Lily wagged her finger. "Don't change the subject. You're going to tell me everything, remember?"

"Not everything." I laughed. "Do you tell me everything?"

A whisper of a smile breezed across Lily's lips. "Fine." She pulled up a stool next to the sewing table and perched on the very end, leaning her cheek into her cupped hand. "Why don't you tell me about how you survived all those years without Mr. Wever."

"Oh." Max shook his head. "That's a sad, sad story."

"Mom's not going to keep the sad stories from me anymore, are you, Mom?" Lily looked to me for affirmation and I gave a curt nod, hoping that Max would realize that my newfound honesty with my daughter still came with boundaries. He gave me an almost imperceptible wink.

"Well," he said. "If that's the case, I suppose I should start by telling you that it was very, very hard to live without your mother for so long."

Lily looked skeptical. "How did you do it? Everton is a pretty small town."

"Necessity is the mother of invention," Max said. "Or so they say. In our case, Elena and I invented a lot of excuses. If we pulled into the grocery store parking lot and noticed your mom's car there, we suddenly remembered that we had to stop by the bank or the post office before we got groceries. Or if we saw her across the park, we would have an irrepressible urge to walk in the opposite direction."

"You did that?" I asked, shocked.

Max straightened up and looked me square in the face. "What choice did we have, Rachel? Cyrus helped us understand the gravity of the situation very early on."

Lily's eyes darted between us. "What do you mean?"

"Dad forbid me to see Max and Elena," I told her. "He knew that they didn't approve of our marriage, and he didn't like that."

Lily looked like she was about to say something, but she checked herself. "I guess we'll get to that soon enough. But right now I think I want to start at the beginning."

"You mean like: 'In the beginning God created the heavens and the earth'?" Max selected a red-handled scissors from the old coffee can that housed a handful of the tools of our trade. "You'd better get comfy—this is going to take a while."

"Nah." Lily reached for the scissors and pulled the fabric that Max had just pinned toward her. He had taught her to make straight, careful cuts and she had become an indispensable part of our suit-making process. "You don't have to go back quite that far. I just want to know about my mom. What was she like when she was my age?"

The wrinkles around Max's eye deepened as he grinned. "Well, now, that's a fun topic. What was your mom like at your age...?"

"Mousy," I said. "Mousy and quiet and knobby-kneed and ugly."

Max regarded me with narrowed eyes. "She's wrong," he told Lily. "It's true, your mother was quiet, but there was nothing mousy about her. She was sweet and artistic and lovely. Actually," he rapped a knuckle lightly beneath Lily's chin, "she looked just like you. The first time I saw you it was like I was twenty years younger and meeting your mother for the very first time."

"Really?" Lily sounded hopeful. "You think I'll grow into these teeth someday?"

"Undoubtedly." Max laughed. "You'll be every bit as beautiful as your mother."

I tried not to roll my eyes. "Flattery will get you nowhere," I said. "I know the truth."

"I don't think that you do." Max tapped his nose for a moment, eyes far away as he thought. "Tell you what," he said to Lily. "I'll give you a glimpse into your mother's world that I think will explain a lot."

"I'd love that." Lily nodded enthusiastically.

"Be careful, Max," I warned. "Is it your story to tell?"

He looked affronted. "Absolutely. It's the story of the first time I ever saw you."

Max wasn't the only one who remembered the first time we met. He and Elena moved into the house next door when I was in second grade, and though I can clearly re-call the day, it never stood out in my mind as an important event. I was only eight years old, timid and uncertain of my place in the world, and I didn't pay much attention to the elderly couple with a garage tailor shop. What did I know about men's suits? My father rarely wore one. The closest thing he had to a suit was a sport coat with patches at the elbows and a collar that seemed unusually broad. He wore it on Sunday mornings, but every other day of the week he donned faded blue jeans and work shirts with frayed cuffs and stains that refused to come out.

But whether or not I treasured the advent of the Wever family in my life, it was an episode that apparently meant a lot to Max. He recounted it with obvious fondness, and as he blessed Lily with details that he unwrapped like small gifts, it hit me that my surrogate father loved me long before I ever even knew his name.

The day that Max and Elena moved in was a postcard-perfect Saturday in May. One of the things that sold them on the house was a half-moon formation of three Japanese cherry blossom trees in the front yard, their spindly branches drooping beneath the weight of pink blooms that sweetened the air of the entire neighborhood. As the Wevers moved in—with the help of a small church group—they considered the warm fragrance of flowers a profound grace: It seemed to soften the blow of moving to a new town at a stage in their life when they were supposed to be firmly planted, not uprooted.

However, before they had unpacked half of the moving truck, it became evident that the center cherry blossom tree was heavy-laden with more than just spring blooms. There were a pair of bare, pale feet poking from the bottom of the blushing canopy. Max said that he kept sneaking peeks at the ten small toes, the slender ankle that from time to time made an appearance.

As the final items were being lifted from the back of the moving truck, Max realized that whoever was attached to the pair of feet in the tree had been there for a very long time. True, he had been in and out of the house and couldn't be entirely sure that the tree-climbing trespasser hadn't shimmied down the trunk and disappeared for a quick snack or a bathroom break. But he felt confident asserting that the child who sat so still among the branches had spent the better part of two hours doing exactly that: sitting quietly in a tree. What sort of a child could do that?

He found out quickly enough. While Elena passed out glasses of cold lemonade, a woman emerged from the house next door. She was wearing a pair of fashionably ripped jeans and a tank top that slipped off her shoulder to reveal the black bra strap beneath. Max was about to call out a friendly hello when he realized that the woman seemed slightly unsteady on her feet. Unsteady, and angry.

"Rachel? Rachel!" The woman shouted from the front steps, angling her face one way and then another. "Rachel Anne, you come home this instant! I don't know where you are but when I get a hold of you . . ."

Max battled his conscience as he tried to decide what to do. Should he alert his furious neighbor to the dangling toes in his tree? Or protect the little girl's hiding place? It was obvious she didn't want to be found.

But the woman on the steps of the house next door was clearly the child's mother, and she had to be worried sick about her daughter. That was undoubtedly why she was yelling, why her face was rosy with the evidence of her fury.

"I'll be back in a minute," Max told Elena. The entire

moving crew was watching the woman with thinly veiled curiosity. "I think I know where her daughter is."

"We all do," Elena said, shaking her head a little. "I just pity the child when that woman finds out."

Max strode purposefully across the lawns, cutting through the trees almost directly beneath the spot where the girl was still crouched. Without moving his head he chanced a brief glance among the branches and spotted a huddled form against the trunk. She had pulled her legs up against her chest and her arms were wrapped tight around her knees. Max caught the impression of hair that matched the dawn and eyes like a summer sky. Limbs as skinny as the branches she clung to. Then he was past and had to turn his focus to the agitated stranger next door.

"Hi," he said, extending his hand as he approached. "I'm your new neighbor. The name's Max Wever."

The woman looked him up and down, and it seemed she was unimpressed by what she saw. "I'm looking for my daughter," she said, forgoing any manners or introductions. "Have you seen a little brat about this tall?" She held her hand up at chest height, then rethought her assessment and lowered it a bit.

The yes was on the tip of his tongue, and it almost spilled right out. But at the last second a breeze swirled between them and Max caught a whiff of something so sickly sweet it was nauseating. All at once he knew that the high color in the woman's cheeks was not fear for her daughter's well-being, it was the telltale rosacea of an alcoholic.

"You're looking for your daughter?" Max repeated dumbly.

She glared at him. "I have to go to the grocery store," the woman said slowly and loudly. She obviously thought he was hard of hearing. "I can't exactly leave her home alone, can I?"

Max was alarmed at the thought of this woman driving. Especially with a child in the car. "Can't it wait? Will your husband be home soon?"

She rolled her eyes. "No, it can't wait. And no, my husband won't be home for another hour or so."

"How old is your daughter?" Max asked.

"Eight."

He could tell she was getting more and more agitated, and he was starting to dread the thought of the moment when the little girl's hiding place would be discovered. Thinking fast he said, "Your daughter's name is Rachel, right?"

She nodded.

"How about my wife and I keep an eye out for her? We can watch her while you're gone."

"I don't even know you," the woman said. But she smiled all the same. "You trustworthy?"

Max put a hand over his heart. "I'll treat her like my own."

"Fine." The woman fluttered her fingers and turned to go. "When she turns up, you tell that little snot-nosed horror that she's getting the spanking of her life when I get home. You tell her that."

Max didn't respond. He couldn't. But the woman didn't wait for an answer. He watched as she stumbled to the garage and got in her car. She backed out of the driveway without incident, but Max determined right then and there that the first thing he would do when she was out of sight was call the cops. His neighbor was obviously a menace.

On the way back to his own house, Max walked below the trees again. He wanted to say hello to Rachel, maybe to even coax her from her perch with the promise of lemonade. But when he found her between the branches, her eyes were squeezed shut tight. She looked like a wounded fairy in the tree with a twig stuck in her hair, a pixie of a thing with shallow wrinkles in her young forehead and the weight of the world on her narrow shoulders.

He wanted to reach up and pull her down. But he didn't. The way that Rachel held herself told him that she wanted to be left alone.

CHAPTER 9

MITCH

December 24, 1:00 P.M.

The Christmas tree in the lobby of The Heritage Home is a fifteen-foot monstrosity. It took a team of four maintenance men an entire afternoon to set it up, and the better part of the following day was spent stringing lights and trimming the prickly evergreen. Mitch knows that he must have walked past it dozens of times, but as he wanders through the lobby on the afternoon of Christmas Eve, he is gripped by the desire to bask in the glow of a thousand points of light. The day is dark already, the sky heavy with snow, and the tree in the center of the warm room radiates comfort. Mitch could use a little comfort.

The scent of pine is heavy in the air, and the tree seems to tremble in anticipation. In reality, the soft waver of the branches is the result of ceiling fans turned on low, but there is something magical about the tree all the same. Mitch stands before it, looking everywhere at once. Trying to take it in. After a minute he notices that there is a little placard in a gilded frame that hangs eye level at the very center: Many of the decorations you see are from our guests' family trees.

When Mitch reads the simple rhyme, he studies the hodgepodge of ornaments with renewed interest. There are antique baubles of paper-thin blown glass. And hand-painted Santas with plumes of cottony beards. But the decorations that cause him to linger, the ones that make his heart stumble, are the homemade offerings. They're by far the best—the paper stars with gobs of glitter and fat, gluey fingerprints, and foil garlands with uneven edges cut by child-safe scissors. Scattered across the sweeping boughs of the tree, there are even a few ornaments that boast pictures of children. Little boys with freckles on their noses and gap-toothed grins. And girls like fallen angels, their halos tipping to one side as they brush mud off skinned knees.

Mitch pores over each face, trying to discern if she is

among them. Did she once labor over a papier-mâché manger for him? Did she smile as a Sunday school teacher snapped a Polaroid for the center of a finger-painted wreath? He can't remember.

"Did you find yours?" Cooper asks from somewhere behind him.

Mitch absorbs the question with nothing more than a slight shake of his head.

"It's one of the prettiest," Cooper says. "At least, I think so."

"Is it homemade?" Mitch wonders.

"Yes." There is a smile in Cooper's voice. "Let's see if you can find it. It's about as big as the palm of my hand, and it sparkles."

It's not much of a description, but something glitters at the edge of Mitch's memory all the same. For just a second he can see it cradled in his hand, a gift that took his breath away. He scans the tree, his eyes skipping over ornaments in their haste to find the one that is his. The one that might lead him a step closer to her.

Mitch can't picture the decoration, but he knows what it is not. He walks slowly around the tree, trailing his hand against the very edge of the needles as he disregards reindeers made out of pipe cleaners and exquisite Russian antiques. Just as his throat begins to tighten in defeat, he catches a glimpse of iridescence a bit above his head. He reaches for the source of the soft glow and plucks it from between the branches.

"You found it," Cooper says softly. "I knew you would."

The ornament is light as air and almost as delicate. It is a single, hand-cut snowflake made from silver paper and glazed with thick shards of white glitter that sparkle like glass. It must have taken hours to plan each careful snip of the scissors, and even longer to carefully coat the slender spires in such delicate strands of glue. Mitch turns it over in his fingers, and as he does a few flakes of glitter whisper free and fall to the floor like snow.

"I'm ruining it," he says, and is surprised to feel panic clutch at his chest.

"No, you're not." Cooper comes to stand beside him. "It's well-worn and well-loved. You've had it for over twenty years."

"Twenty years? Has it been that long?"

"She's a grown woman now."

Mitch twirls the snowflake by the silver string attached to the tip as he spins this information around in his mind. Twenty years? She's grown up without him. He's lost so much time . . . Suddenly, he has a thought. He looks up at Cooper almost hungrily. "Will she come? For Christmas, I mean?"

Cooper's eyes shift to the tree. "I don't know, Mitch. Maybe."

"Does she visit me?" Mitch is too confused to be wary. For all he knows she comes every week and he exhausts her with his constant questions. Maybe his own faulty memory is driving a wedge between them that he doesn't even know about. "Have I just forgotten her?"

"You haven't forgotten her," Cooper says, ignoring Mitch's first question. "You mix things up sometimes, but I guarantee you: You have not forgotten your daughter. Not for a single day."

"Can I call her?" Raw hope is written across Mitch's face. "Maybe if I call and invite her, she'll come."

Cooper seems to consider this for a moment, but before Mitch can get too excited, Cooper puts a steadying hand on his arm. "Why don't you write her a letter? Sometimes the best way to express how we feel is to put our thoughts down on paper."

"But . . ." Mitch fumbles, disappointed.

"I'll help you." Cooper smiles encouragingly. "You can dictate and I'll write. I have very nice handwriting. It's almost legible."

Mitch sighs. "Mine isn't?"

"Not really."

"What will I say?"

"I'm sure you'll come up with something."

Feeling like a bit of a thief, Mitch takes the paper snowflake with him as he follows Cooper into the atrium. The open space has cleared out a bit; many of the residents are taking a much-needed rest after lunch. But Mitch isn't tired. In fact, his fingers vibrate with energy, and it's all he can do not to race over to the table where Cooper is obviously headed. For the first time in a long time, he feels like he has a purpose. Something he must do. A letter is a brilliant idea. He wonders why he never thought of it before.

"Make yourself comfortable," Cooper says, indicating a table near the window. "I'll go get some paper and a pen. Would you like a cup of tea?"

For once, Mitch doesn't have to wonder at his own preferences. "Coffee," he says definitively. "Black."

Cooper grins. It was a trick question. "Of course. Be back in a few."

The chairs at the table are plush, but Mitch doesn't feel like sitting. Instead, he wanders the length of the atrium, watching the snow fall just outside the glass. It's been accumulating for hours now, and the world is blurred with white. Mitch is surprised by a sudden longing to play in it, to run outside and throw himself against the snow and watch as the flakes dance like stars around him. He'd like to lie in it, facing the sky, and let the muted light settle around him like a blanket.

But of course he can't do that. They would think he was even crazier than they already do. Maybe they would lock him in his room, or fit him with one of those straitjackets that he can, for some unfathomable reason, see so clearly. How can he know what a straitjacket is, but not be able to recall his grown-up daughter's face? Life is cruel, Mitch decides.

And yet, it's beautiful, too.

He knows that life is beautiful because he holds the evidence in his hand. In spite of the indistinct haze of guilt that he feels whenever he thinks of his past, Mitch knows he must have done something right. Something good. Nothing else could merit the priceless gift he holds in his hand. When he looks at the snowflake, the care with which it was constructed, he knows beyond a shadow of a doubt that for a while at least the girl who wielded the scissors loved him.

"Did I fail you completely?" he asks the little snowflake. It seems like a tiny piece of his daughter, a glimmering extension of the child she once was. But the paper doesn't answer. It merely sheds a few more flakes of glitter.

Mitch presses the snowflake against the cool pane of glass before him and lets his gaze drift to his own watermark reflection. He still has a full head of hair, but it's so white it disappears in the fringe of snow. His eyes are milky, too, soft and lined like overripe fruit. I've gone to seed, he thinks. I don't know how to be old.

It's an excuse, and Mitch knows it. Just like all the other ones. I didn't know how to be a father. I didn't know how to raise a daughter. I didn't know how to make it better, how to stand between my wife and the little girl that she terrorized for all those fragile years.

And yet, even as Mitch thinks these things, as he comes to grips with the fact that he failed, he is shaken by the fierce realization that he's not gone yet. Maybe it's not too late.

"I'm going to tell you everything I felt. Everything I should have said," Mitch says. He cradles the snowflake in his hands, touching each fragile tip with the soft pad of his fingers. "I just pray it's not too late."

As he turns the ornament over and over, Mitch notices something for the very first time. It's a smudge of dark along one narrow spire on the back side of the decoration. Even before he squints at the mark, he knows that the streak of ink is a message of sorts, something she left behind. Maybe it's her name scrawled in a childish hand. Or maybe a Bible verse, something that will jog his memory.

Mitch has to bring the snowflake almost to his nose to make out the minuscule inscription. And then he has to read it four times before it sinks in. It feels like a cipher, a secret code that was written just for him. Just for this moment.

I remember.

"I remember, too," Mitch whispers.

CHAPTER 10

RACHEL

October 16

The Kempers family lived in a picture-perfect little house situated in what most people in Everton referred to as the "old" part of town. In some places, the original brick roads peeked through concrete that had been poured over top, and ancient trees created a canopy that intertwined above lazy streets. I loved the collection of storybook houses with dormer windows and dizzyingly steep roofs. Every home boasted a unique characteristic, from wrought-iron shutters that were a century old to picket fences painted a bright and cheery white.

Sarah's home was distinct because of the exquisite garden that filled the entire front yard. Her flowers started at the overflowing window boxes beneath her dining room window, and extended all the way to the edge of the sidewalk. And beyond, I noticed, as I stepped over a browning black-eyed Susan that had sprouted from a crack in the cement. It was too late in the season for her, and yet she clung to life. Apparently Sarah's green thumb could not be contained by something as silly as a slab of poured concrete.

Even though I was on a mission, I couldn't help but smile as I mounted the steps to Sarah's front door. Her fall mums were bursts of brilliant color that seemed to match her personality: bold, vibrant, and unapologetic. But when Sarah swung the door open before I could ring the bell, I had to rethink my final assessment of her. She didn't look unapologetic. She looked absolutely heartsick.

"Sarah!" I was shocked to see her so distraught. She was normally so effervescent it was almost maddening. "Is something wrong?"

She stepped outside into the mild fall day and let the screen door slam behind her. "I didn't sleep at all last night. I just feel so terrible about what happened at the coffee shop! Can you ever forgive me? Sometimes I let my mouth get ahead of me, but I didn't mean to—"

"It's okay," I said, putting my hand on her arm to stop

the barrage of words. "I came over here to apologize to you. I shouldn't have reacted the way that I did."

"Oh, you had every right to react that way. I absolutely blitzed you with my half-baked assumptions ... and in a public place! What was I thinking? I am without a doubt the world's worst pastor's wife."

I grinned in spite of myself. "Is there a handbook? Do they hand out awards for pastors' wives?"

"I'm sure they do. Somewhere there's a committee that's divided into seventeen subcommittees that undoubt-edly monitor our every move. The good pastors' wives—the ones who play the piano and have perfected the art of baking bread for communion—get a gold star for every good deed. And when they add up all those gold stars . . ." Sarah twisted her lips and gave a wry shrug as if to say, "You know what happens then."

"You've given this a lot of thought," I said, laughing.

"You have no idea. When I married David I told him that I would make a terrible pastor's wife. He didn't listen to me."

"He thinks you're perfect," I assured her, although that was probably an understatement. Anyone who had ever seen the two of them together knew that David Kempers had eyes only for his remarkable wife. And who could blame him? Even when she came rushing down the center aisle at church, five minutes late for the Sunday morning service and clutching her ten-year-old twins by the hand, she wore a smile that lit up the room. She was magnetic, a force to be reckoned with. And no one knew that better than her husband.

I was surprised by a twinge of jealousy. Was there ever a time that Cyrus adored me the way David would forever adore Sarah? I doubted it. In fact, I doubted that anyone had ever loved me with that sort of abandon.

"Well," I said, suppressing a sigh, "I guess we both screwed up. Anyway, I really am sorry. You're one of . . ." I was about to say my only friends, but that sounded so pathetic I couldn't make myself finish. Besides, I had the rest of the women in our Bible study. I had Max. And Lily.

But Sarah finished the sentence for me. Only she tweaked it in the most wonderful way. "You're one of my best friends," she said, giving me a quick, fierce hug. "I'm sorry I hurt you."

"Best friends?" I repeated before I could censor myself.

"Of course." Sarah backed away and met my eye almost gravely. "You're not like everyone else, Rachel. Don't get me wrong, the ladies we hang out with are nice and all, but don't you sometimes feel like they're . . . fake?" A horrified look seized her pretty features. "Did I just say that out loud? I told you I'm a terrible pastor's wife."

"I won't tell a soul," I reassured her. "But if you want to talk about fake, you're in the presence of the queen. My entire life is one big fraud. How can you imply that I'm anything other than the absolute worst kind of liar?"

"That's different." Sarah shook her head, her mouth puckered in disapproval. "You don't try to pretend that everything is perfect, you just keep to yourself. The reason I finally brought up Cyrus is that I thought that's what you were waiting for: I thought you wanted someone to notice."

I had to consider that for a moment. Was I really hoping for someone to reach out to me? To look closer and realize that my shiny life had nearly rusted through? "I guess you're right," I finally said. "I don't know why, but I feel like I can't go on pretending anymore. That's why I came clean with Lily, and why I'm working for Max . . ."

Sarah's eyes went wide at the exact moment that I realized my mistake. No one knew that I was working for Max. No one was supposed to know that I was working at all.

"You can't tell anyone," I said desperately. "Cyrus doesn't know, and if he found out—"

"I promise," Sarah cut in. "Not even David. But who's Max?"

The question pulled me up short. "Who's Max?" I repeated, wondering how in the world I could begin to describe the man who had saved me once and was in the process of doing it again. I couldn't. It was too hard. "I guess you're just going to have to meet him," I said.

Sarah linked her arm with mine. "How's now for you?"

I looked at the knot of our elbows, the soft pink floral of her sleeve over the clean navy of my sweater. They complemented each other beautifully. I smiled. "Now is perfect."

Max and Sarah hit it off immediately. Within minutes of walking through the back door, Sarah had Max laughing at one of her jokes. And by the time Lily dropped in after school, Sarah was fully committed to our project and had learned to wield a fabric steamer with admirable flourish.

"I can't sew to save my life, but I sure know how to blow steam!" she said, laughing at her own terrible pun.

As for Lily, she had always liked Sarah, and she greeted my friend with a warm hug and a barrage of questions about the upcoming Christmas play. Our church was doing a live Nativity with a horse-drawn sleigh and hot cider, and Lily was angling for the part of the angel. Rumor had it David had worked out a way to float an angel from the haymow of the barn where the Nativity would be staged to the double-wide door of the stable. Lily wanted to fly.

"I don't know," Sarah teased. "Are you angel material?"

"Definitely not." I pulled the end of Lily's ponytail and gave her a wink.

"Oh, I don't know about that." Max gave me a knowing look over Lily's head. "Her mother is pretty good at making angels."

"Who? Me?" I touched my fingers to my chest. "To the best of my recollection, I've never made an angel in my life. Though I will concede that my daughter is angelic."

"You're right about Lily," Max said. "But you're wrong about making angels. You used to do it all the time. In fact, Elena once snapped a photo of one of your angels. I think I have it around here somewhere . . ." Max turned from the sewing table and began to search among the papers of the cluttered bulletin board that hung above the desk. There were pages from magazines, pizza coupons, and orders, but in between the bright rectangles of paper there hung a few random photographs. I could make out a black and white copy of the Wevers' wedding portrait, and another taken on some mountain vacation. Elena looked young and pretty standing in a meadow with her arms stretched toward the horizon.

Max finally found what he was searching for half-hidden behind a restaurant napkin that had been scribbled with a man's measurements. He took out the thumbtack and studied the photograph for a short time before he smiled to himself and held it out to me. "See? You used to make angels."

At first, all I could see was white. It seemed Elena had taken a picture of light itself. But in a second my eyes adjusted, and I realized I was looking at bright whorls of snow. The sun was shining furiously, casting each snowflake into vivid relief so that I could almost see every unique design. And someone had mounded up all that snow with the sweep of arms and legs. It was carefully shaped into the perfect outline of a feather-winged angel.

"A snow angel," I said, and was surprised to realize that I had spoken aloud.

"You made lovely snow angels," Max confirmed. All over your front yard, and sometimes over ours, too. Elena took that picture one morning after a particularly big storm. You must have been out there in the middle of the night, because when the sun broke through the clouds the next day there was a company of heavenly hosts all over the neighborhood."

"What a gorgeous thought!" Sarah came to look over my shoulder. "Oh, I just love it. Lily, I think you have to be the angel. It runs in your family."

Lily pulled on my forearm and brought the picture down so that she could see it, too. "You made snow angels?" she asked, wonder in her voice.

"Don't sound so shocked," I said.

"Well, it's just that after hearing some of your stories, I didn't think you ..." Lily fished around for just the right wording, then gave up with an apologetic shrug. "I didn't think you had much fun as a kid. I didn't think you did stuff like that."

"Like play in the snow?"

She wrinkled her nose. "I guess not."

I stalled for a minute, going through a mental list of the childhood memories I had shared with my daughter. Max had told her about the first time we met—when I had hid in the cherry tree for hours to escape my mom. And I had recalled the blue dress incident, my first batch of failed cookies, and a few other doomed affairs that chronicled my mother's verbal and emotional abuse and my father's busy schedule that left little time for me. But had I told her about anything positive? Anything that would cause her to believe that my younger years held even a glimmer of grace?

The truth was, there wasn't much to tell. I had friends, but I could hardly remember their names. And I'm sure that there were times that transcended the stark reality of my days, but they were overshadowed by my own broken heart. What could I say to Lily?

"I thought that night was a dream," I admitted quietly. "I remember making snow angels, but I thought that I had dreamed it."

"It wasn't a dream," Max said. "I saw you out there. The night you littered the neighborhood with angels."

"You did?"

Max nodded, and though his mouth held the shape of a little smile, his eyes were sad. "There was a huge snow-storm, and when I heard voices outside I was worried that someone's car had gotten stuck. But it was just you. You and your dad. I'm not sure I've ever seen you look so happy."

Something vicious ripped through me at the mention of my dad. A desperate longing, a desire to go back to a time when my hand disappeared completely in his. Those days were too short, too fleeting, and the pain that had built up between us seemed insurmountable. And yet, for just a moment all of that fell away. Nothing mattered but the fact that on the very night that I needed him most, he was there.

My mother was unusually harsh that night. I don't remember what I did or what she said, but I do know that she was angry enough to hit me. I was far too old for spankings, though I had endured the shame of that particular punishment much longer than I should have. But at a willowy eleven years old I already stood as high as my mom's shoulder, and no matter how furious she was, spanking was obviously out of the question. So she slapped me.

It was a rather pathetic attempt at discipline, and her open-handed smack across my cheek was weakened by her intoxicated state. But it stung all the same, and tears sprang to my eyes even before she turned away.

"Go to your room," she barked. But that was the last thing she had to tell me. I couldn't wait to escape.

The room was cold, and frost formed on the darkened window in patterns that dipped and curled. I shut the door behind me and paused with my hand on the lock. It would feel so good to make the quarter turn that would close me in an impenetrable fortress, but I didn't dare. Bev hated it when I bolted my door, and I knew that if she came to continue our argument and found herself locked out it would only stoke her fury.

I settled for climbing into my bed fully clothed and pulling the blankets up to the tops of my ears. Only my eyes poked out, and as I lay in the long shadows of a winter night, I watched the world outside my window for some sign that everything would be okay. All I could see was frost.

She had yelled at me before. She had hit me before. But something about the abuse that night burrowed deep inside me and leaked a slow, sad poison. Usually I could close myself off, exist in some quiet, inner place where I had the strength to breathe in and breathe out—to ignore what she had done. Not that night.

I tried to cry quietly, but each sob was torn from some secret place that held tight to such troublesome emotions. Soon I was burying my face in the pillow, trying to muffle the sound of my heart breaking for what had to be the hundredth time. I don't know how long I huddled there in the dark, but by the time my tears began to wane it was hours past dark.

When a creak of bedsprings alerted me to the fact that I wasn't alone, I whipped around, terrified that my mother had come to tell me to shut up. But instead of Bev, my dad sat on the edge of my bed. He was still wearing his work clothes, and he smelled of sawdust and metal. In the dim twilight of my bedroom, I could see the lines around his eyes, and a small, fresh cut high on his cheekbone. Even in the pit of my suffering, I wondered what had happen to cause the bright graze.

I tried to ask, but my throat was closed tight.

It was Dad who spoke. "Oh," he sighed. "Oh, Rachel. I'm so sorry."

I wasn't sure why he was sorry. Bev had hit me, not him. But he looked like he was in pain, and when he reached for me I closed my eyes for fear that I might cry harder still.

My dad was not an affectionate man, so I was shocked when he peeled back the blankets and lifted me into his

arms as if I weighed nothing at all. It didn't cost him anything to support my seventy-pound frame, but I felt like
he had pulled me from the wreckage of my childhood. I
buried my face in his chest and clung to him as if I was a
toddler instead of the young woman I believed I was.

We stayed like that for what felt like an age, the passing
of one era into the next. I savored the feeling of being cradled in my daddy's arms, his head bent over mine, forehead
resting against my crown. When I was finally calm enough
to hear the beat of his heart as it thrummed against my
temple, I wondered how long it had been since he had last
held me. Years, at least. Had he ever hugged me with such
tenderness?

Dad was distant. Distant and busy and forever tired
from the long hours he spent at work. Every once in a
while he would catch Bev berating me and he'd give me
a quick, guilty glance. I suspected that he knew he should
do something to stop her, but he didn't know how. So instead he avoided me. He avoided us. But this—this stolen
moment that began with his heartfelt apology—made up
for all of it. Almost.

I didn't want to break the spell, but when Dad realized I
was over the worst of it, he gave my back an awkward pat.
"It's snowing," he said.

It had been snowing all day. "I know." I sniffed and ran
the back of my hand over my eyes, my nose. And with

that, the magic was gone. My back was stiff and I was uncomfortable. I wiggled a bit and tried to remember what it felt like to feel so safe, so loved in the circle of his embrace.

"Your mother is asleep."

I shrugged a little.

"Let's go outside." It was a strange, sudden request, and at first I thought he was joking.

"Outside?"

"You should see it, Rach. The snow is still coming down, and in the light of the street lamps it looks like the stars are falling from the sky. I feel like making a snow angel."

I pushed back from his chest and regarded my dad with disbelief. "You want to do what?"

"I never taught you how to do that, did I?" He looked positively crestfallen at the thought. "In all these years I've never played in the snow with you. Not once. Every little girl should play in the snow with her daddy."

"I know how to make a snow angel," I told him. But it was the wrong thing to say. His mouth slipped into a forlorn little frown. I tried to soften the blow. "I could . . . I could show you if you'd like."

Dad closed his eyes and nodded. He swallowed hard. "I'd like that very much."

We didn't bother with snow pants or any of the other winter gear that I'd usually don to play in the snow. Instead, we zipped on our winter coats and stuck our feet in boots, and crept into the winter wonderland like thieves. And I suppose we were stealing something: a few minutes away, a memory of our own. In the midst of all that was our dysfunctional family, it felt decidedly extraordinary to be doing something so normal. We were nothing more than a daddy-daughter pair on our way to kick up the new-fallen snow.

We tromped through the front yard, carving knee-deep tunnels in the powder-soft snow with our boots. It was perfectly still, and the flakes tumbled straight down, as big as silver dollars. They collected on our sleeves and anointed our heads with white halos that glowed in the gentle light of the dim street lamp. I held my arms out and studied the cool dusting of ice.

"It's really pretty," I said.

"Beautiful."

I snuck a peek at Dad, but he wasn't looking at the snow. He was looking at me.

Dad cleared his throat and motioned to the snow around us. "It won't hurt if you fall, Rachel. Not tonight. Just let go. I'll pick you up."

So I did. I spread my arms out wide and tilted back until gravity had its way. There wasn't a moment of hesitation in my descent, and when I hit the snow it puffed around me and drifted softly over my cheeks. I didn't expect the sweet cushion of the fall, and I couldn't stop the giggle that escaped my lips as I flung my arms and legs. I felt like a very little girl. Carefree. Light as air. Indescribably happy.

Dad kept his promise. When my snow angel was done, he caught me around the middle and plucked me from the center of my design so I didn't have to ruin the white perfection with my footprints. We did it again and again, all over our yard and beyond, and each time I fell Dad lifted me from the snow so that it looked like each careful pattern was the result of some delightful enchantment.

After we had littered the neighborhood with our divine gifts, Dad reached for my hands one last time. My cheeks were flushed but my fingers were frozen, and as he pressed them in between his giant palms, he gave me a mysterious smile. It was layered and complex, happy and bittersweet, hopeful but filled with regret. And then he did something so surprising I believed for years to come that I had dreamed up the entire astonishing night.

He bent and kissed my cheek. He whispered, "You are my angel."

CHAPTER 11

RACHEL

October 20

With Cyrus in California, Lily and I decided to have a sleepover. We gathered her lavender pillow and a handful of teddy bears and watched a princess movie in the king-sized bed I shared with her father. Cyrus would have been furious if he knew that I spread a bath towel over the bedspread and painted Lily's toenails in the flickering light of the TV, but for once I didn't care. After reliving my snow angel memory, I was exhausted and dazed, tingling with emotions I hadn't felt in a very long time.

It helped to listen to Lily's gasps and giggles as

a preteen beauty found her on-screen prince. But it was even more therapeutic to know that when my daughter remembered her childhood, it would be blessedly devoid of the drama I had endured. I had worked hard to give Lily a happy, stable life, and as I watched her lovely profile, I knew that I had succeeded. At least, in part.

I played in the snow with my daughter. Baked her cookies, told her she was beautiful, painted her toenails. And though Cyrus was far from the ideal father, he didn't hurt Lily—physically or otherwise. He more or less left her alone. But with the truth of my one precious father-memory still stinging the frayed edge of my soul, I was sorry that Lily would never know that sort of love. Even if it was as brief and temporary as an extinguished flame.

"Lil?" I asked when the credits were rolling. "Are you happy?"

My daughter turned to me and crinkled her nose. The delicate dusting of freckles across the bridge rose and fell. "Of course, I'm happy. I have purple toes!" She waggled her feet at me.

"I don't mean about your toes, I mean . . ." But I didn't know how to say what I meant. It was too big, too heavy for someone so young.

Lily seemed to sense my hesitation. She crossed her legs beneath her and regarded me seriously. "There is something that would make me very happy," she said carefully.

"What?"

"I'd like to meet my grandpa."

A sad laugh burst from me before I could stop it. "Honey, I haven't seen your grandpa in years."

"Why?"

Why indeed. It was a sticky, impossible question and I didn't know how to answer it. How far back did I have to go to find the place where our roads diverged? How could I explain that sometimes a thousand little things added up to something so big it had the power to crush a relationship? If I tried to tell Lily about every small argument and misunderstanding, they would seem like nothing at all. But when I stacked them all side by side, they became an unscalable wall.

Never mind the fact that I had made my choice long ago. When Cyrus swept in like my personal Prince Charming, my dad seemed to automatically fall into the role of the wicked stepfather. In the light of the impossible romance that was kindled, everything my dad did and said was cast into shadows and suspicion. Did he have my best interests in mind? Had he ever? My bitter, teenaged heart was still torn from the knowledge that my dad chose my mother over me. So I chose Cyrus.

I sighed. "Honey, it's been too long. I couldn't go back, even if I wanted to."

"Why not?"

Kneading my forehead with my fingers, I tried to come up with a way to explain that Cyrus had forbidden me to see my own father. He called my dad a blue-collar grunt, the sort of white trash that a Price simply couldn't be associated with. Of course, I was naive and eager to believe anything that my newfound love declared to be true, but when I thought back to those pivotal years I was ashamed that I bought Cyrus's ugly opinions of my family hook, line, and sinker. How could I admit that to my daughter?

"Why can't I meet my grandpa?" Lily pressed. "You asked me if I was happy, and I'm telling you that this would make me happy. I want to meet him."

"When I asked you if you were happy, I wasn't talking about your grandpa. I was talking about your dad."

"What does Dad have to do with this?" Lily looked confused.

"Everything!" I threw up my hands, exasperated. "I've tried so hard to give you a good life. To spare you from the sort of childhood that I had. But no matter what I do, I can't be everything for you. I can't be a dad."

"And you can't be a grandpa."

I dropped my forehead in my hands and moaned. "Fine, Lily. You're right. I can't be a grandpa."

She was quiet for a long minute, then I felt her shift on the bed. When I looked, Lily had flopped back on her pillow and was staring at the ceiling. "Maybe you have to stop trying to be everything," she said. "And stop trying to do everything."

"Isn't a perfect life a happy life?"

"There's no such thing as a perfect life," Lily said seriously.

"Don't I know it." I sank back into my own pillow and rolled on my side to face my daughter. "Have I failed you completely? Will all of this come out in counseling someday?"

She giggled. "You bet. But, no. You haven't failed. I just want what I've always wanted: the truth. I can take it, Mom."

"You've been getting it. Big, fat doses of the truth. It's ugly, isn't it?"

"Sometimes."

"And you still want it?"

"Always." Lily tucked her hands beneath her cheek and stared at me with eyes so big and deep they seemed bottomless. "I'm not afraid. Besides, God is my shield. You don't have to be."

I bit my bottom lip and considered the wisdom and maturity of my amazing daughter. "Where did you hear that God is your shield?"

"It's in the Psalms."

"And since when do you read the Psalms?" The Prices

were a churchgoing family, always had been, but we weren't the scripture-quoting type.

"Sarah has devotions before pageant practice. Yesterday she talked about that passage. It's a promise. Sarah says God is my defender and deliverer."

"I thought I was."

Lily just blinked.

"Okay." I reached out and smoothed a piece of hair from her forehead. "I get it. You're growing up. You're strong and grounded and amazing in every way. And you're old enough to know why you can't see your grandpa."

"I am?"

"Apparently." I blew a hard breath through my nose. "I didn't think you were. But I guess I've been wrong about a lot of things."

My mother's death rocked me to the core, and not just because it was so unexpected. In the wake of her accident, I battled a dozen different emotions, from grief to shock to something I was much less inclined to acknowledge: relief.

I could hardly even admit to myself that one of the side effects of Bev's passing was the gradual lightening of the cloud that seemed to perpetually hang over me. The house was empty without her, cavernous even, but there was an undeniable peace in the echo of those silent rooms.

It was summertime, my father's busiest work season, and since I had nothing at all to occupy my time, I spent several days after Bev's funeral holed up in my room, confined to the only space where I had previously felt safe. The four walls of my bedroom were a security blanket of sorts, a place where I could hide—and even lock the door, now that my mother was no longer around to forbid it.

I don't remember exactly when it happened, but there came a point that I realized my self-inflicted captivity was totally unnecessary. I could go wherever I wanted to go. Do whatever I wanted to do. At a fragile fourteen years old, it was a dizzying, thrilling, terrifying thought.

My first foray into the world without my mother was far from earth-shattering, but it changed the entire landscape for me. One afternoon I emerged from my bedroom and surveyed the dusty clutter of our outdated living room. Everything seemed fuzzy and stale, and though I blinked my eyes to clear the haze, the picture didn't change. So I picked my way across the crumb-littered carpet and pulled back the heavy curtains. The day outside was bright and clean as polished glass, downright blinding to my unsuspecting eyes.

Since Bev didn't like to have the windows open, it took

me a while to coax the rusting lock to turn. It eventually let loose with a wooden exhalation, a creak that seemed to say, "Finally." I threw the double-hung pane as high as it would go and watched as the warm breeze from outside transformed my living room. The fresh air filtered into every corner, exposing all the places that time, and my mother, had forgotten.

It took me the rest of the afternoon to clean our living space. I filled an old ice cream bucket with warm, soapy water and wiped down the walls. Then I dusted and carefully moved every stick of furniture into the dining room. It was an exhausting endeavor, but I was determined, and I managed to exile everything but the couch. When the room was empty, I vacuumed for an hour at least, scouring carpet, baseboards, and even the blades of the ceiling fan. It was suppertime before I stepped back and surveyed my handiwork.

Nothing was the same. I had ripped down the heavy curtains and left only a light, bamboo shade in their place. And everything was rearranged, from the furniture to the outdated knickknacks that populated the tables. It looked like a different room. A different room in a different house. There wasn't even a hint of my mother in the new, sunny space. It was exactly what I wanted.

Dad came home before dark. I knew that there was a lot more work for him to do at the construction site, but since Bev's passing he felt obligated to be home for me as much as possible. That included awkward, nightly suppers around the big table in the dining room. Someone from the church brought over a different meal every night, but whether we dined on lasagna or chicken casserole, it all tasted the same to me.

I didn't mind the time alone with Dad, even if it was somewhat uncomfortable. He was always tired from work, his eyes heavy-lidded and his shoulders slumped, and though he tried to make conversation with me, it felt forced. But the day I cleaned the living room I antici- pated his homecoming with an almost giddy excitement. I was sure that he would love it—that he would see what I had done and understand what it meant: I was ready to move on.

When I heard my dad's car in the driveway, I pushed myself up from the couch and smoothed the cushion where I had been sitting. Everything looked crisp, and I placed myself at the very center of it all so I could see his reaction when he came up the stairs. I held my breath as I heard the front door open and close, followed by three quick thumps as he took the steps two at a time.

The moment his head peeked above the half-wall be- tween the living room and the entryway of our split-level house, Dad froze. "What have you done?" His cheeks were tanned and leathery from all the days he'd spent in the sun, but even beneath the glow of his dark skin I could see that he had paled.

"I ... I cleaned the living room," I stammered. "Everything is spotless. It's rearranged ..." But, of course, he could see that with his own two eyes. Nothing remained the way that it had been. Nothing.

"What have you done?" he repeated, as if he hadn't heard me. "Where are your mother's magazines? Where is our family photo?"

"I kept everything," I said. "I just moved it around. Got rid of some of the clutter."

"Where is the jar of sand that your mother had on the coffee table?" Dad surged into the room and circled the coffee table almost frantically. "Where is it? Your mother got that sand on our honeymoon. She carried it all the way back from Oregon in a plastic grocery bag!"

"It's on the counter," I whispered, pointing in the direction of the kitchen. "I didn't know where to put it."

Dad disappeared in a couple of big strides and emerged from the kitchen a second later with the jar of sand clutched in both hands. "Put it back where it belongs," he said, and I was surprised at the anger in his voice. "Put it right here." He slammed the jar down on the table so hard I thought the glass would crack.

I swallowed, tried to make amends. "I was just trying to—"

"Erase your mother?" He interrupted me so abruptly I was left with my mouth gaping open. "Look at this place! It's as if she never existed. Do you know why she had the couch at that angle?" He didn't wait for an answer. "So she could stretch out and watch TV. Or why she liked the window closed? So that we had some privacy." Dad stomped across the room and shut the window with a bang.

I wasn't used to being yelled at by my dad, and I was stunned to find that it didn't affect me quite the same way that Bev's shouting always had. Maybe it was because I was sick and tired of being screamed at. Maybe I just felt strong after the hours I had spent purifying my home and my heart. Either way, when my dad raised his voice at me, I raised mine right back.

"I've been cleaning for hours!" I shouted. "This place is a pigsty!"

Dad looked taken aback at my tone, but instead of backing down he only dug his heels in deeper. "Clean all you want," he said, "but don't you dare touch your mother's things. Have a little respect."

"Respect?" I choked. "You want me to respect her?"

"Of course I want you to respect her! She's your mother, for heaven's sake."

"Well, she wasn't a very good one." I was sobbing now, but my tears were born of fury, not sorrow. The injustice of all the years that I endured her verbal and emotional assaults was hitting me with the force of a train. I was breathless and shaking.

"How dare you?" My dad's words were indignant, but his tone was splintered by pain and disbelief. "How can you say that?"

"Dad . . ." I held out my hands, questioning. "She hurt me. You know that."

He shook his head. "All mothers and daughters fight."

"This was different, and you know it."

"Your mother was an amazing woman."

"She was an alcoholic." I didn't really know what an alcoholic was, but I had heard more than a few people whisper it at the funeral. They said that my mom was drunk when she died, but that Dad wouldn't let the hospital do a tox screen, whatever that was. And whether or not I could define the terms I heard floating around like debris from the wreckage, I was certain that they revealed much about my mother. They helped me to understand a bit of the whole. They carried an indelible weight.

Dad must have felt it, too. "You don't know what you're talking about," he said through clenched teeth. "Your mom went through a lot. She suffered a lot. And it's not fair for anyone else to judge her. Especially you."

"I'm not judging her," I cried. "I just want you to admit the truth."

"What truth?"

It was such a simple question, but with those two little words I knew that no matter how hard I tried to convince him, Dad would never accept who Mom was or what she had done. For reasons I couldn't begin to fathom, he felt a deep-seated need to protect her, to gloss over the messy parts of our past. The places where my mother's ghost still haunted me. What truth? he asked. Before that night, I thought there was only one. My mother was abusive. But Dad loved her because he knew why.

"Forget it," I whispered. I pushed past him and would have run to my room, but he caught me by the arm and stopped me.

"I want everything back the way that it was."

"Fine."

"And Rachel?"

I didn't want to look at him, but I knew my dad wouldn't continue until I met his gaze. "What?" I said, raising my tear-swollen eyes to his.

"I know you don't believe it, but your mother loved you."

He was right: I didn't believe it. But it was obvious to me that he did. How could we both see the same woman through such different lenses?

As I closed and locked my bedroom door behind me, I considered for the very first time that sometimes truth is in the eye of the beholder. My mother abused me. True. My mother loved me. True? Would I ever know?

Probably not. But there was one thing that was certain: My dad and I had two very different versions of the truth. And I didn't know if I could ever forgive him for refusing to concede that my childhood up to that point was the battleground where my mother chose to fight her personal demons. That night, a chasm split the earth between my dad and me. A separation that, in the years to come, would lead us further and further apart. That would lead him right out of my life.

Or maybe I walked out of his.

CHAPTER 12

MITCH

December 24, 3:00 P.M.

Mitch has a headache. It's dull but persistent, a thick band of pain that begins somewhere at the base of his neck and extends all the way up and around where it throbs in his forehead.

"I don't want to do this anymore," Mitch mutters. There is a man across from him, hand poised over a sheet of lined stationery. Words fill the paper with the dip and sweep of careful penmanship, the sort of writing that is a dying art. They don't teach kids cursive anymore. At least, Mitch doesn't think they do. But the man with the defined jaw and delicate hands writes beautifully, and it seems as if he's waiting for Mitch to say something before he goes on. The tip of the fountain pen is a hair's breadth from the paper.

It irritates Mitch, the way the man looks up expectantly. "You were just telling me about the first time you met Bev. About the diner...?" The man reaches for a piece of stationery that is lying facedown beside him. He scans the page before he finds the right spot. "Here: 'She was the most beautiful woman I had ever seen. But she had built a wall around herself. She had a reputation for being hard, heartless even, but I knew that she was hiding something. I took one look at her and knew that she was scarred. I saw her. And I loved her. What else could I do?'"

Mitch stares at the man.

"You're kind of a poet," the stranger says, smoothing the page. "A true Renaissance man."

"I don't know what you're talking about." Mitch feels dizzy, and angry. The anger boils up from somewhere deep inside of him, a place that is dark with confusion and things left unresolved. He doesn't know how to respond, or why this man is looking at him with such sorrow and pity mingled together.

"It's okay," the man says. He takes the thin stack of papers and taps them against the table so that all the edges line up. Then he folds them together and tucks them inside an envelope. He seals it. Dates it.

"What is that?" Mitch growls.

"A letter."

"Who's it for?"

"Someone who I hope will appreciate it very much."

Mitch knows that people usually don't appreciate what they've been given until it's too late. But he doesn't say so. Instead, he pushes back from the table, suddenly desperate to get away from the man who still sits across from him. There are memories that linger in the air between them. Things unspoken. Mitch grasps at understanding, but it slips through his fingers like mist. It's exhausting, and he wants nothing so much as to be far from this man and his antiquated penmanship.

"I'm going to my room," Mitch announces. "I want to be alone." But he stalls a few steps from the table because he does not know where his room is. The atrium where he is standing is vaguely familiar. He feels more or less safe here, like he should know it well. And he also knows that he has a room somewhere nearby, a place he can escape to. The problem is, he can't remember what it looks like or which direction he should go to find it.

"I'm down the hall from you," the man says, appearing beside Mitch. "We can walk together."

Mitch can't fight the tremor that shudders through him at the proximity of the man. He knows this person, or should know him. It's a sick, terrifying feeling to accept that he's forgotten something that should be second nature. He feels defeated, betrayed by his own mind.

"I'm Cooper," the man says quietly. Reminding him. "Let me walk you to your room."

Although he wants to grumble and fight, Mitch forces himself to step back and allow Cooper to take the lead. Cooper does so graciously, moving away without a backward glance, sparing Mitch's pride as much as possible. He can't imagine anything quite so humiliating as being led around like a puppy on a string.

Mitch's room is down a long hallway in the middle of a dozen matching doors. Cooper lightly touches the frame with his fingertips and nods without turning around, then he continues to the very end of the corridor and disappears into his own sanctuary. Mitch watches him go. Once he is alone, he stands on the threshold of his room and peers inside, curious and more than a little afraid that it will be as foreign to him as everything else.

It is. The room is small and sparsely appointed. There's a narrow bed tightly made with neat, hospital corners, a faded rocking chair, and a table under a wide window. The bathroom is just inside the door, and it smells of bleach and industrial soap. It could be anyone's room, but while Mitch doesn't recognize it, he does know that it's his. There is a picture of a little girl propped against an anemic-looking plant on the table, and his reaction to it is almost visceral. It's her. And he belongs here.

Mitch shuffles into the room and closes the door firmly behind him. He looks for a lock, but there is none, and he battles an impulsive desire to push the table against the door to ensure that he won't be bothered. But it seems like more work than it's worth, and besides, he's not sure he could move the table on his own. He'd only be setting himself up for more indignity if he was bested by a piece of furniture.

The room is cool, and Mitch notices that there is a robe hanging from a hook on the back of the bathroom door. It's ratty and off-white, but he pushes his arms through the sleeves anyway as he makes his way to the table, where he picks up the photograph. It's dog-eared and curled at the edges, but her face is still as fresh and sweet as ever. Mitch presses the picture to his chest with one hand and extracts a snowflake from the pocket of his cardigan with the other. For some reason he knows that the glittering ornament is there, and that it belongs beside the image of the ginger-haired little girl.

There. It's a reunification of sorts. A tattered, mis-matched memory that evokes nothing in him so much as a bottomless yearning, the sort of ache that could easily swallow him whole.

Mitch lies down on the bed with the photo and the snowflake, one clutched in each hand, and stares up at the ceiling. He feels hollow and empty, his chest caving beneath the weight of a regret that he cannot name. But it is real and razor-sharp. He can't ignore it. He can't wish it away or pretend that it doesn't exist.

When the nurse's aide slips quietly into the room, Mitch doesn't stir. But he's not sleeping, and she seems to know that instinctively. She speaks quietly to him, and he tunes her out until she's standing right beside the bed.

"Your medication, Mr. Clark?" It's phrased as a question, but she is holding out a tiny paper cup, waiting for him to sit up and take it.

"What is it?" he asks.

"The same medication you're given every afternoon."

"What is it?" Mitch repeats. He wants specifics.

"Something to help you calm down. To help you sleep tonight."

Perfect. If she offered, he'd gladly take a painkiller, too, but he's not sure that an analgesic would take the edge off the pain that he's feeling. Mitch pushes himself into a sitting position and places the photograph in his lap so that he can accept the paper cup. Inside is a single white tablet, and he tips it onto his tongue. There is a bitter sting in the place where it rests until the nurse offers him a glass of lukewarm water and he washes it down.

"Good job." She smiles and nods as if he is a little boy. "Would you like to take a nap before supper? Should I put this on the table?" Her fingers brush the edge of the photograph, and Mitch snatches it away.

"No," he says forcefully. A part of him wants to shout at her for even daring to touch it, but he's too tired to be combative. Instead of fighting, he falls back. He doesn't even argue when she pulls the blankets up to his chest.

Mitch hears soft footsteps and the click of his door falling closed. Then the only sound in the room is his own heartbeat in his ears. He is utterly and completely alone. Abandoned. He's sure that he's never felt so lonely in all of his life, and yet he doesn't even know who it is he longs for. Her, he decides, clutching the photo to his chest. Mitch wishes she would walk through the door, ponytail swinging, a half-smile quirking the corner of her perfect mouth.

But even as he wishes it, he knows it is an impossible dream. She's not coming. And in the dim shadows of his sterile room, Mitch begins to cry.

CHAPTER 13

RACHEL

October 22

Cyrus was gone for ten days. Ten glorious, drama-free days during which I hardly gave him a second thought. Lily and I flung open the windows to let in the brisk, autumn air, and lived like we didn't have a care in the world. It was pizza in the living room for supper and a box of doughnuts leaning against the counter for breakfast. I even caught Lily drinking orange juice straight out of the container one afternoon. She gave me a guilty look when I stuck out my hand for the juice, but she dissolved in giggles when I put the jug to my lips and took a few long gulps myself.

Our afternoons with Max took on an almost lazy air, since we were halfway done with the order and it wasn't even November. Instead of working, working, working, we made sure our hands were busy, but we also talked and laughed, and one day Max surprised us by taking a new bolt of cloth out of the back room. We were used to the dark, rich fabrics that would become Max's suits, and the soft pleats of Elena's dress material that still hung around the shop served as a reminder of the woman we were missing. But this cloth was entirely different.

It looked vintage, though it had to be new. The subtle pattern spun swaths of cream and mint in a swirl that even at first glance I could tell was tailor-made for Lily's exquisite coloring. It seemed as if God had blended those colors just for her.

"What's this?" Lily asked when Max handed her the bolt of cloth.

"It's not much now, but it's going to be a dress."

"For me?" Lily couldn't keep the excitement out of her voice.

"Yes, for you. I thought you and your mom would enjoy working on it together."

"It's kind of a summery fabric," I said, taking a corner between my fingertips. It was smooth and breezy, light as air.

"So it will be a warm-weather dress." Max shrugged. "Take your time. We have plenty of it."

I wasn't so sure that he was right about that. Our secret weeks together were a reprieve, a sabbatical from a life that was steadily strangling me. It was wonderful and unexpected, filled with the sense that there was something looming just out of sight. Something that made my fingers tingle and my heart beat fast, but the more practical side of me felt sure that this interlude would come with a staggering price tag—it would cost me dearly. And the day of reckoning was surely just around the corner.

The night before Cyrus came home, I had a premonition of his return. I woke up well past midnight, hot and shivering at the same time. "It can't last," I said out loud. My voice seemed to boom in the empty house, and I clapped my hands over my mouth as if I had uttered a curse. It felt like a curse to me. I didn't want Cyrus to come back.

When I woke up that morning and went downstairs to take a shower, my husband was standing in the kitchen. He looked rumpled from travel, and he was rubbing his neck with his fingers, trying to get the kinks out. His back was turned to me, and I watched him for a moment, searching for the man that I had married in the lines of his broad shoulders.

He was there, maybe. The young man I had fallen in love with. The boy who was the perfect mix of child and man, who made me laugh. Who made me feel as if every atom in my body had been plugged in to an electrical current whenever he was around. I still tingled in his presence, but looking at him in the thin, early morning shadows that fell across our kitchen, I realized that it was a different kind of power that made me tremble now.

"You're home," I blurted out, fearful that he would turn and find me standing there. Staring.

Cyrus swung his head around to regard me, then closed his eyes and went back to massaging his neck. "I'm exhausted," he said. "And my neck is killing me. Come here." He motioned me to follow him as he took a seat at the small breakfast table in a windowed nook just off the kitchen.

I stopped a few feet away from him, wondering what exactly he wanted from me. But I didn't have to wonder long. Cyrus leaned half out of his chair to grab me by the wrist and yank me a couple of stumbling paces so that I was standing beside him. Then he took my hand and put it on his neck.

"That's the spot. Not too hard."

"You want a neck rub?" I asked.

"No, I want an omelette." His tone was thick with sarcasm that I chose to ignore. Early on in our marriage Cyrus loved nothing more than to remind me of where I came from: a blue-collar family where my father didn't make enough money for my mother to stay home. He knew that Bev had worked long hours at the truck stop, and it was a source of constant derision. No Price woman would ever be allowed to subject herself to such humiliation, but Cyrus sometimes reminded me that even though I didn't bring home minimum wage, my life was that of a short-order cook: He ordered, I jumped.

I tried not to sigh as I tightened the belt of my robe and placed my hands on either side of my husband's muscular neck. Cyrus was obviously tapped out from his cross-country adventure, and I was fairly certain that he would use the rest of the day to catch up on sleep before heading in to work tomorrow. It was a depressing thought. If he was home all day, I had to be, too. That meant no Max, no Sarah, and no time alone with Lily. How could I get a message to Max without Cyrus finding out about it? I didn't want to leave him hanging.

"Anything happen while I was gone?" Cyrus's question startled me.

"Uh, no," I stammered. "Nothing interesting anyway." Nothing that I can tell you about.

"Aren't you going to ask me about my trip?"

My fingers paused in their ministrations, but I recovered quickly and hoped Cyrus didn't notice. "Of course. How was your trip?"

"Long. That's why we drove through the night last night. Jason wanted to get home."

I didn't ask Cyrus if he wanted to get home, too. I knew

the answer to that question. The conversation stalled for a minute as I tried to think of something else to say. We had become so bad at communicating that I didn't even know where to begin. What was I supposed to say to the man who had fallen out of love with me? Had he ever been in love with me?

Before I could formulate an acceptable query, I heard the thump of Lily's footsteps on the stairs. It was too early for her to be up, but by the drum of her quick pace I could tell that she had woken up with an idea, something that made her pulse pound high and hot. I spun toward the arch that framed our open staircase, praying that Lily would realize that her father was home before she said something that she shouldn't.

I wasn't quite so lucky. "Mom!" Lily called, halfway down the steps. "I know what I want to do! I know how I want to use Ma—" She stopped abruptly at the foot of the stairs. "Dad. You're home."

"Just got back," Cyrus said. I could feel his shoulders tighten beneath my hands. "What were you saying, Lil? Just now? 'I know how I want to use mmm ... ?'" He drew out the M, leading Lily with a tilt of his head. He nodded for her to finish.

Lily's eyes shot to mine, and I was devastated to see real fear in them. I knew what she was going to say, or at least, I could guess. She had been on the verge of telling me that she knew what she wanted to do with Max's material. I had encouraged her to pick out a pattern quickly so that we could get started. But she was torn between three styles and couldn't make up her mind. Of course, she couldn't say any of that in front of Cyrus, and I witnessed all of her excitement fizzle away as she realized the implications of her father's presence in our kitchen. She wasn't a very good actress, especially under duress, and for a few seconds I was convinced that she would cave right then and there and tell Cyrus everything.

"Rachel, seriously?" Cyrus jerked away from me and rubbed his neck with the heel of his hand. I realized that I had been pinching him, and my face flushed. Lily and I were as guilty a pair as ever there was, and if Cyrus didn't know something was up, he had to be both stupid and blind.

"Sorry," I muttered, mentally preparing myself for the fallout.

But as I watched, Lily gained control of herself and managed to give Cyrus a winning, if lopsided, smile. She looked adorable in her pajama pants and T-shirt, hair mussed from sleep and cheek wrinkled by the crease in her pillow. Though I was scared half to death, it was nearly impossible not to grin at her.

"Welcome back, Dad," she said, crossing the kitchen in her bare feet. For a moment it looked as if she was going to give Cyrus a hug, but that would have been so uncharacteristic as to be downright ridiculous. She stopped her-self. "I was going to say, I know how I want to use my money."

"Money?" Cyrus asked suspiciously.

"Mom gave me ten dollars to help her clean out the flower gardens and I know how I want to use it."

It was true, I had given her ten dollars to help me win-terize the gardens. But I was so blown away by her quick cover that my mouth dropped open all the same.

"I want to take you and Sarah Kempers out for ice cream," Lily continued. "This afternoon."

"What makes you think your mother and Sarah deserve ice cream?" Cyrus's words were light, joking even, but as he stood he shot me a calculating look. He definitely knew something was going on.

"Sarah kept us company a bit while you were gone," Lily said. It was a risky move, an admission that came dan-gerously close to the truth. But after her near slip on the stairs, there wasn't an ounce of hesitation in her bearing.

"Lily's right," I chimed in. "We've been spending some time with Sarah. She's been great."

"The pastor's wife," Cyrus said, more to himself than to us. I could tell that he was looking for an angle to exploit, something that would give him permission to forbid us to see her. But apparently he couldn't find any fault with our growing friendship, so he shrugged. "Whatever," he said, yawning so wide his jaw cracked. "Just be sure to get the fat-free stuff. No wife of mine is going to be a blimp."

I was still trying to figure out how we had gotten off so easy when Cyrus moved past me. He turned around at the last second and pulled me roughly to him, giving me a kiss that was anything but tender. It took my breath away, but not for good reasons. And when he finally broke away, Cyrus's eyes bored into mine, searching for answers that I prayed he wouldn't find. "I don't like secrets," he said, each word no louder than an exhalation. Then louder, so that Lily could hear, he said, "I sure am glad to be home. A man's home is his castle."

Since I knew I wasn't Cyrus's queen, I guess that made me his prisoner.

I called Sarah almost immediately after Cyrus went to bed for the day. Because I couldn't be sure if he was listening on the other line, I tried to keep the conversation perfectly innocuous, but I could tell by her tone that Sarah realized the gravity of the situation.

"I'm so glad Cyrus made it home safe," she said. What she meant was, What are we going to do?

"Me, too. But I'm afraid I'm going to have to cancel

our meeting this morning. I should be home if Cyrus needs me."

"Of course. I'll let everyone know." *I'll tell Max you're not coming.*

"Oh, and Lily wanted me to ask you if she can take us out for ice cream after school. You know, as a thank you."

"Sure. I'll ask David if he can keep an eye on the twins. Shall I expect you at three?" *I'll be counting the minutes . . .*

The day seemed to drag on forever, and when I pulled up at her house a little before three, it struck me that Sarah thought so, too. She was waiting for me on the sidewalk, pacing up and down as if she couldn't keep still. The moment I stopped, she slid into the passenger seat of my car and leaned across the console to give me a squeeze. "Hey," she said. "How are you doing?"

"Fine." I smiled thinly. "But I don't know how I can keep going to Max's. Cyrus definitely suspects that there's something going on."

"Did he . . . ?" Sarah's eyes searched mine, but she couldn't bring herself to finish.

"Did he hit me?" I said. "No." I glanced over my shoulder and pulled away from the curb, angling the car toward Lily's school. "It's fine, Sarah. Really. Everything is just fine."

"No, it's not!" Her vehemence surprised me. "Come on, Rachel, you know everything is not just fine. Look at you:

You're scared. And you can't see Max . . . Don't you get it? This isn't okay."

"Of course I 'get it,' " I said coolly. "It's my life, remember? I'm living it."

"Sorry." Sarah sighed. "I'm not very good at this. It just drives me crazy that he has such power over you. And honestly, I don't understand why you let him have it."

"I don't expect you to understand. I expect you to be my friend."

"I am your friend."

"You're also a pastor's wife," I reminded her. "And marriage is supposed to be sacred. How can you counsel me to go against my husband's wishes?"

Sarah put her hand on my arm, but I kept my eyes on the road. "Rachel, listen. Marriage is sacred. And the Bible says that God hates divorce. He hates it because he wants better for you. He never intended for you to have a broken marriage or a broken home. He loves you."

I made a little sound in the back of my throat because even though I did not doubt Sarah's sincerity, I doubted her message.

"Oh, don't do that," she said softly. "I don't care what Cyrus has made you believe. You are beloved."

It was very hard not to roll my eyes. What did I know about love?

But Sarah didn't push me. Instead, she changed tack.

"You're not safe, Rachel, and neither is Lily. Cyrus needs help, but I don't think he's going to come to that realization on his own."

I almost laughed at the thought of Cyrus admitting that he needed help. I believed that God still performed miracles, but in all my years of marriage, I had been given no indication that there was one forthcoming. And yet, was it wrong to hope?

"You sound like my dad," I said dryly.

"Your dad?"

I hadn't even realized I had spoken aloud. I waved my hand as if to rid the air of my words. "He used to say that all the time. That Cyrus needed help."

"Your dad sounds like a wise man."

My cheeks flushed with shame and I rushed to change the topic. "Maybe Cyrus will change," I said hesitantly.

"Maybe you have to give him the opportunity to."

I bit the inside of my cheek, considering all the things I could say to her. But we didn't have time for a philosophical conversation—I was already pulling up to Lily's school. I put the car in park and gave Sarah my full attention. "I know you're my friend. But I need you to understand that I don't take this lightly. I feel very, very trapped, and I don't know how to get myself out of this mess. It's too big. Too complicated."

"But don't you think if we just—"

"Hi, Mom," Lily chirped, swinging open the back door and flinging herself into the seat. "Hi, Sarah."

We both pasted on smiles and abandoned our heated discussion. "Hi, honey," I said. "Where to? This is your show."

"Ice cream," she said firmly. "I want to go to the Dairy Stop before it closes for the winter. And I want to eat it at Oak Grove."

"The lady knows what she wants." Sarah winked at me. "Who are we to argue?"

We all got soft-serve, twist cones from the Dairy Stop, and then I made the five-minute drive to the park. Oak Grove was a little nature reserve with hiking trails and secluded corners for romantic picnics that squatted in the low hills just a few miles outside the Everton city limits. It was the perfect place to be alone, and I could guess why Lily chose it: She wanted to be able to talk freely.

I drove down the winding, tree-lined road and parked on a gravel turn-off near my favorite trail. It was an unusually warm late October day, and though the trees were stripped and bare, their leaves littered the ground ankle-deep. We crunched down the path, kicking up leaves and losing our way. But I knew where we were going, and eventually we came around a bend and were afforded a view of our destination: a giant slab of basalt rock that sunned itself on the side of a hill.

The rock was as large as a house and rose in jutted columns that were perfect for climbing. I had taken Lily here many times before, and she ran the rest of the distance, then scrambled up and away toward her favorite spot, half-eaten ice cream cone still clutched in one hand. Sarah followed with a laugh, and soon all three of us were stretched out on a smooth, flat section, enjoying the way the black stone was warm beneath us.

"Thanks for the ice cream cone," Sarah said, nudging Lily with her shoulder. "It's just what I needed today."

"The Dairy Stop closes on Friday," Lily told her seriously. "We have to go five whole months without soft-serve ice cream."

"And Dairy Dogs," I sighed.

"And chili cheese fries."

"It's a tragedy," Lily confirmed. And in spite of the tight knot of fear that existed where my heart should be, I loved the fact that my daughter thought the temporary closure of a mom and pop roadside stand was a tragedy.

We were quiet for a few minutes, licking our cones and watching the way feathery strands of high, white clouds trailed across the stark blue sky. I wished that we could just remain in this place of silence, of peace, but when Lily swallowed her last bite of cone, she turned to me with a decidedly businesslike air.

"So," she said. "What are we going to do now?"

"You mean now that Dad's home?"

She shook her head. "Now that he suspects something. I saw that look in his eye. He's going to be watching us like a hawk."

"Max is just going to have to finish without us." I tried to sound indifferent, but I couldn't keep the regret out of my voice.

"He can't," Sarah piped up. "I stopped by there this morning after you called and he looked positively heartsick. We still have five full suits to go and the order needs to be shipped by December 1. Max can't do it alone."

"He's got you," I reminded her. "You can help."

"I'm hopeless," she argued. "I can run a steamer, that's about it."

"So he'll be a little late."

"Mom." Lily gave me a dismayed look. "It's Mr. Wever's last order. He's counting on that money for retirement. You know that. He can't work anymore with Mrs. Wever gone."

"What would you have me do?" I cried. "If Dad finds out he'll go ballistic. And you're right, he knows we're up to something. It's just a matter of time."

"Maybe you can take a little break. Stay away from Eden for a week or two, then when Cyrus lets his guard down you can go back and help Max finish," Sarah said.

I bit my lip, considering. "That might work."

"It's our only choice." Lily nodded as if that settled it. Then she twisted her mouth into an anxious little bow. "It is our choice, right? I can still come, can't I?"

I hated to do it, but I had to. I shook my head. "I'm so sorry, honey. I can't drag you into this. If your dad finds out what I've been doing, that's fine. I can deal with it. But if you're tangled up in it . . ." I could hardly bring myself to consider the possibilities.

"That's not fair!" Lily's attempt at fury was thwarted by the tears that instantly sprang to her eyes. "You can't stop me from seeing Mr. Wever!"

"It's not what I want either," I said, reaching for her. But she yanked away from me.

"Then do something about it! I don't get it. Why don't we just leave?"

It was a question I had asked myself a hundred times since the day I said, "I do." Am I done yet? Is it time? But is the time ever right to leave your spouse? The man who swore to love and protect you, even if he broke those same vows in a thousand different ways?

Although it seemed unbelievable, even to me, I could come up with a list a mile long of all the many reasons to stay. My daughter deserved a daddy, even if he wasn't going to win any dad of the year awards. Besides, I had nowhere to go, nothing to do. My whole world was the tiny town of Everton. And if I left, everyone would know that my entire life had been a sham. Really, life with Cyrus wasn't that bad. It's not as if he regularly beat me or anything like that. He called me names. Every once in a while he was more forceful than necessary. It was nothing I couldn't handle.

As I mentally went over my laundry list of reasons, I came to the bottom of my logic, to a place that I hadn't visited in many, many years. Somewhere, buried in a forgotten corner of my heart, I came to the unexpected realization that some small part of me still loved my husband. Feared him, yes, but whether the memory was fresh or not, there was a time that he looked upon me with a gaze so filled with passion it took my breath away. And there was something inside me that still longed for that: for someone to love me the way that Cyrus did back when he first fell in love with me. I hadn't imagined it, had I? We had been in love once.

Maybe, if I stayed, he'd remember.

I fell in love with Cyrus at my senior prom.

It was an accident, something that I never intended to happen. But I was raw and reeling from a fight with my dad, and I suppose that even if it had nothing to do with love, I would have fallen one way or another that night.

Sometimes, the only thing to do when you're hurting is to let yourself go headlong.

My dad had given me money to buy a prom dress, but when I came home with a gown that made me feel like a princess, he made me feel like a slut.

"You can't wear that," Dad said when I came out of my bedroom in the pink, strapless sheath.

"Why not?" I smiled, sure that he was on the verge of teasing me. Perhaps he would say that I looked too pretty, that I was bound to steal some poor guy's heart. I knew that the blush of the dress was perfect for my skin, that it made my hair glow like fire.

"Because it's totally inappropriate."

"What?" My smile quirked a little. It wasn't quite the response I expected.

"It's . . ." Dad fumbled for words, but I could see that he wasn't amused.

I smoothed the fitted waist with my palms, confused. "It's not too tight, is it?"

"It's too tight, too low, too revealing . . ." Dad fanned his hands as if he could hardly stand the sight of me. "You can't wear it."

"What?"

"You are not going to wear that dress. I won't allow it."

A wave of hurt washed over me, but before I could

drown in it I felt a strong, unexpected undertow of fury. It was a lethal combination. "Excuse me?" I bit off the words even as I choked back tears. "It's a beautiful dress."

"The dress is fine—"

"So it's me?"

"No," Dad sputtered. "It's you and the dress. You in the dress." He closed his eyes and shook his head as if to clear it, and when he looked at me again there was steel in his expression. "You may not wear the dress. That's final."

"What am I supposed to wear?" I nearly shouted.

"Find another dress."

"It's too late to find another dress! Prom is less than a week away. I'm lucky I found this dress."

Dad thinned his mouth into a hard line and turned away from me. Apparently the conversation was over, but I was still left standing in a dress that I had believed only minutes before was the most gorgeous thing that I had ever had the good fortune to wear. When I had tried it on in the store, I didn't even care that I was going to the prom solo. Who needed a date when I had a dress that made me look like a movie star?

"Do you want me to stay home?" I cried. "Is that it? You want to ruin it for me?" Dad stiffened, but he didn't rise to the bait. I tried harder. "Or maybe you can't stand it that I actually look pretty. You always wished I was a boy, didn't you? 'It's so hard being the single father of a daughter . . . ' At least, that's what you tell your friends. Maybe you'd like it better if I wore a tux to the prom!"

Dad shook his head sadly, but instead of arguing with me, he left the room. I teetered in the middle of the living room floor, my high heels sinking in the shag carpet, and felt a surge of defiance so powerful I was stunned at my own capacity for rebellion. All my life I had been a fairly compliant child. Easy to manage, if a little prone to random acts of disappearance. But suddenly it was as if all my years of quiet obedience had finally burst the seams of self-control. I was tingling, heartbroken, and downright livid.

If Dad refused to let me wear the dress, I'd give him exactly what he wanted.

I wore a suit to the prom. One of Max's nicer suits, a mohair-wool blend in a gray so soft it was almost silver. There was a faint, pinstripe weave, and Elena helped me dart the back of the coat so that it cut sharply against my tiny waist and outlined my figure. We paired it with a slim-fitting lilac dress shirt, black heels, and Elena's mother's pearls. My self-confidence had never been very healthy, but as I spun a slow circle in front of my mirror, I had to admit that the effect was striking.

Even Max thought so. He had been hesitant to lend me one of his suits, but when he realized the only statement

I was trying to make was one of independence, he reluctantly agreed. When I was finally all ready to go, hair piled on my head and wisping down in face-framing curls, Max laughed and gave me an impulsive hug.

"Who says modesty is dead?" he said. "You look beautiful. Professional and poised. As if you are on your way to conquer the world!"

I felt like I could conquer the world. The suit was a far cry from the pink dress, and though I still mourned that particular loss, I believed for a moment that I was on the verge of something exciting and new. I had broken through the barriers of my own self-perception, and the woman I had found was strong and self-possessed. Capable of anything.

My confidence didn't falter in the presence of my peers. I had been a wallflower all my life, but all at once I was the center of attention. All over the decorated banquet hall, people talked about me behind their hands, and not in a bad way. The girls seemed to approve of my unorthodox ensemble, and more than a few guys shot me an admiring wink.

One boy in particular appeared transfixed. Cyrus Price, the football superstar and most popular boy in school, had graduated the year before but everyone knew that his girlfriend would be crowned Prom Queen. So he had come home from college for the weekend just to accompany his small-town sweetheart to a rather pathetic high school prom. All I had to do was glance at him to know that he was bored to tears and regretting his decision to leave behind his exciting college life for this provincial pageantry. But as I peeked, the handsome Cyrus caught my eye and something in his countenance shifted.

His look burned me. I felt myself flush and I quickly turned away, directing my attention to the couples on the dance floor so that I could calm my racing heart. But a few minutes later when I gathered the courage to sneak a second glance, Cyrus was still watching me. He smiled a little, the corners of his mouth lifting in what could only be considered invitation.

I didn't dare to look at him again.

The evening was almost over when I felt a hand trail lightly across my shoulders. I shivered and looked up, sure it was one of my friends. But Cyrus stood over me, the bow tie of his tux rakishly crooked and a knowing smirk on his face. "May I have this dance?" he asked, offering me his arm.

I opened and closed my mouth a few times, uncertain if he was being serious or if he was merely playing me. "Where's Stephanie?" I finally managed. Surely his girlfriend was hovering in the wings.

"She left," he said simply.

"But . . ."

"Come on." He grinned, revealing a dimple in his cheek. It was agonizingly boyish and endearing. "Don't leave a guy hanging."

Still, I stalled. I didn't know what to do or how to respond, so I cast around, hoping someone would save me or reveal that this was all a big joke. But before anyone came to my rescue, Cyrus leaned down with his hands planted firmly on the table behind me. He ducked his head close to mine. His warm breath stirred the tendrils of hair that fell against my neck and made me shiver. "Please," he whispered. Just that: please.

When he took me by the hands, I let myself be pulled out of the chair and onto the dance floor. Cyrus seemed to find my reluctance beguiling, because he smirked as he curled one arm protectively around me and pressed me close. My chin just fit against the curve of his shoulder, and since we were tucked so close I had no choice but to rest my cheek against his neck. Cyrus smelled of aftershave and spice, a warm, earthy scent that made me feel dizzy. Drugged.

"You're amazing," he exhaled into my ear.

"Do you even know my name?" My voice was high, almost squeaky.

"Rachel Clark. Your mother was a drunk and your father is a loser, but you are the most beautiful woman I've ever seen."

My mother was a drunk? My father a loser? Maybe I should have prickled at Cyrus's casual dismissal of my family, but the truth was, I hardly heard those insults. The most handsome, popular boy in Everton had called me amazing. Beautiful. I heard that one word, and I tumbled head over heels. No matter that I was the goat herder's daughter in Cyrus Price's personal fairytale. He saw that I was a woman, not some little girl who had been hurt by her mother, bossed by her father, and more or less forgotten by the rest of the world. It was like he handed me a new life, and I happily stepped out of the past and into a present that felt very much like a brand-new beginning.

I was too innocent to realize that history has a way of repeating itself.

CHAPTER 14

RACHEL

November 10–November 24

The weather turned suddenly. What had been a mild, beautiful fall was transformed in one stormy night to a vicious winter. An inch of ice reworked the world in layers of glittering glass, and I found my thoughts shifting more than ever to Max. He was no invalid, but I hated the thought of him walking the few short blocks from his home to the shop. He could slip and break a hip, or worse. And though I knew he was a perfectly capable driver, that didn't comfort me much. The roads were treacherous, and I had long ago learned how deadly car crashes could be.

Two weeks into my self-inflicted exile from Eden Custom Tailoring, I broke down and gave Max a quick call. It was the middle of the afternoon and I was idle and bored. The house shone from my frustrated attention and dinners had been elaborate all week. When I finally gave in and picked up the phone, there was a triple-layered carrot cake freshly frosted and dusted with shredded coconut on the counter, and an apricot-marinated pork loin roasting in the oven. I felt so stale and useless I was entertaining ideas of churning my own butter or baking a month's worth of bread from scratch. Something, anything to keep my hands busy.

I decided that, for a few minutes at least, I could keep myself occupied by checking in with my favorite tailor. I dialed quickly and tapped the counter with restless fingers as I waited for Max to pick up.

"Eden Custom Tailoring," he answered on the fourth ring. His voice sounded thin to me, anxious.

"Hey, you." I wished I could reach through the line and give him a hug. "How are you doing?"

"How are you doing?" Max turned the question around on me with all the concern of a loving parent. "I've been worried sick about you."

"I'm fine," I assured him. "Totally and completely fine. Bored. But Cyrus doesn't suspect a thing and I'd like to keep it that way. Give me a few more days . . ."

"Don't come back," Max said. "I'll get the suits done. And if I don't, it won't be the end of the world."

"You'll have to pay back the down payment that they gave you." I knew how Max conducted business, and I couldn't stand the thought of him writing out a check for ten thousand dollars to cover the amount he had already received. I suspected most of that money was already gone, spent on fabrics and overhead. "I'll be there on Monday," I insisted. "We'll get this job finished."

"Please, Rachel. Don't. I shouldn't have asked you in the first place. It was wrong of me."

As much as I hated to admit it to myself, a part of me longed to jump at Max's absolution. He was giving me a gracious way to bow out and go back to a life that was, if not happy, at least predictable. I knew my place in Cyrus's world. I knew how to avoid his pitfalls, and if ever I slipped up it was easily remedied by the sort of punishment I had come to expect. The kind of penance I could handle. Defying Cyrus opened up all sorts of new and frightening possibilities. It changed everything, and I wasn't sure if I welcomed that change.

But as I thought about the last six weeks of my life—the development in my relationship with Lily, the deeper friendship that I had forged with Sarah, and the opportunities that had seemed to unfurl with each day I spent existing in a place where I had grown in confidence and grace—I realized that I didn't want to go back to the way things had been. No, I couldn't go back to the way things had been.

"You know what, Max?" I clutched the telephone tighter, terrified and thrilled at the passion that was billowing up inside of me. "I'll be at your shop tomorrow morning. No matter what."

"But, Rachel—"

"No buts. This has gone on long enough. Cyrus can't keep me from you."

"What are you saying?"

"I think I'm finally done, Max." My skin prickled at the thought. "Not done with Cyrus necessarily, just done with this dynamic. I want my life back. At least, I want one square inch of my life back—I want to be able to spend time with you."

The silence on the other end of the line made me second-guess myself. But before I could press Max for some support, he asked me another question. "Do you think Cyrus will just give it to you?"

"What do you mean?"

"You said that you want your life back. Do you think Cyrus will just give it to you? After all this time?"

"I was strong once," I said. "Remember the night of my senior prom? Remember how I moved out after graduation when my dad told me I couldn't see Cyrus anymore and live under his roof? I knew what I wanted and I went after it. I want to be that person again."

"Sweetheart," Max said, his tone soft but firm, "headstrong is not the same as strong. In both of those instances you were angry and you wanted to prove a point. What are you proving now?"

"That I am my own woman," I spat out. "That I shouldn't have to be scared of anyone. Least of all the man who swore to love and protect me."

"Oh, Rachel." I could picture Max shaking his head. "You are your own woman, and Cyrus should cherish you the way you've always deserved. I want Cyrus to come to that realization almost as much as you do. But I don't think that this is the way to go about it. I'm scared of what will happen if you stand up to him now. I don't think he'll take it as well as you seem to believe he will."

I paused for a moment, trying to envision the conversation I would have with my husband. No matter how I tried to cast it, it wasn't pretty. I hated to admit it, but Max was right. The chains of my life had finally chafed me raw, but confronting Cyrus out of the blue had trouble written all over it. "What am I going to do?" I cried, all of my resolve dissolving in unexpected tears. "I don't want to do this anymore!"

"I know, honey. I don't want you to do this anymore.

But we'll find another way through it. We'll think about it. Make a plan."

"Okay." I swallowed around the lump in my throat. "Whatever happens, I'm coming back to Eden. I'm going to help you finish the order. And that's final."

Max didn't try to argue. "Just be careful."

"I will. I'll see you tomorrow."

We hung up without saying good-bye.

Miraculously, my final two weeks at Eden Custom Tailoring passed without a hitch. Because I didn't know what else to do, I took up the routine that I had abandoned when Cyrus came home from California, and I found that it still fit like a glove. In the mornings, Max and I worked alone. And every afternoon Sarah joined us for an hour or two at least. Everything seemed to be going smoothly, except for the dark cloud of Lily's vehement disapproval.

It broke my heart to ban her from Max's shop, but I didn't feel like I had much of a choice. I couldn't stand the thought of Cyrus finding out about my newfound independence—especially now that I was starting to believe freedom, even a small piece of freedom, was something I was willing to fight for. Fortunately, Lily's obvious frustration could be chalked up to preteen angst. She pouted and shot me the occasional brooding look, but I supposed that sort of behavior was par for the course with most eleven-year-old girls. It stung me, but I knew that we'd come out okay on the other side.

Before I knew it, November had all but disappeared, and Max and I found ourselves carefully packing the last suit between sheets of tissue paper. We had been so busy finishing the job that we hadn't thought much past the completion of the very last stitch. All at once our hands were empty, our sewing machines silent. The shop filled with a quiet so thick it was almost tangible.

"We did it," I said, rippling the stillness with my whisper. As Max slid the top onto the cardboard box, a shocked little laugh escaped my lips. Not only had we finished the order in time, we had kept the secret from Cyrus. It was too good to be true. "I can't believe that we did it."

"I can." Max caught my eye. Pride was unmistakable in his gaze.

I held up my hand for a high-five, but Max ignored my palm and pulled me into a warm embrace. Only a moment before I had been so happy I thought I would burst, but in the circle of Max's arms I suddenly realized that a chapter in our lives was over. This brief interlude, this reprieve from my everyday life, had come to an end. The suits were packaged and ready to go, and Max was officially retired. Eden Custom Tailoring was closing its doors, and my reason for spending time with the man I loved as dearly as a father no longer existed.

"What now?" I whispered against the wool of his thick sweater. He smelled of linen and paper, clean and new like the life that I had pretended to lead while I was protected by the walls of his shop. "I don't want this to be over."

"Me neither," Max admitted. "It has been so good to have you in my life again. I've missed you so much."

"I can't say good-bye like before." I had started to tremble, and Max gripped me by the shoulders and eased me away so he could regard me from arm's length.

"I want to show you something," he said. "But you have to promise you won't be angry."

My brow furrowed, but I nodded slowly because Max looked so desperate, so earnest.

He turned to the desk along one wall of the workroom and opened the middle drawer. Lifting out a box of envelopes and some office paraphernalia, he dug to the very bottom of the drawer and emerged with a single photograph.

"Here," Max said rather unceremoniously, handing me the picture. "It's yours."

I gave him a quizzical look and turned my attention to the slick paper in my hand. It was a photo of me.

The woman in the picture was so young she looked like

a child. Her hair was loose, eyes wide, blue T-shirt stark
against the pale lines of arching collarbones. I felt the air
leave me in a quiet rush, but not because of the way the
photo captured my fleeting youth. Because of the way it
highlighted the bruise.

I was turned away from the camera a bit, and the curve
of my cheekbone as it angled for attention was glossy and
purple. It really was an ugly injury, the sort of mark that
was difficult to look at because I could almost feel the hot,
tender ache of the swollen skin.

"I remember when you took this," I said, tapping the
photo with my fingernail. "You snapped it when I came
to collect my things after Cyrus told me I couldn't see you
anymore. You took several of me and Elena together. But
I don't understand why you kept this one. It's such a horrible picture. You have lots of nicer ones. Prom and wedding pictures . . ."

Max ducked his head. "I kept it because it tells the
truth."

"What truth?" My eyes shot to Max. "I told you I
slipped in the shower."

"That's the oldest line in the book," Max said, shaking
his head. "Along with 'I tripped down the stairs, I fell off
my bike, I slid on a patch of ice . . . ' I think Elena and I
heard them all. And we never believed them. Not once."

"What didn't you believe?" Sarah quipped as she swept

into Eden. Her eyes sparkled as she unwound a scarf from her neck, and her lips were turned up in a breezy smile. She had come with David's pickup to help us transport the boxes, and I was sure that getting caught in the middle of an awkward exchange was not at the top of her priority list. I opened my mouth to change the subject, but before I could utter a word, Sarah noticed the photo in my hand. "Is that you?" she asked, peering over my shoulder.

"Well, yes, but . . ." I trailed off at the look on her face.

"Wow." Sarah's smile had disappeared completely as she studied the stark photograph. "Look at you. How in the world could that monster raise a hand to you? You're nothing but a child."

I was so used to covering for him I didn't even flinch. "Cyrus didn't do anything," I said almost indignantly, but the lie screamed like fingernails on a chalkboard. In that instant, something inside me shifted and I felt the full weight of my life and what it had become. "Oh." I whispered. I don't know if it was the look on Sarah's face or the fact that she was right—that the woman in the picture was hardly more than a little girl. Either way, I think I understood for the very first time just how bad things really were. "Oh, no."

Sarah put an arm around me and bent her head to mine so that our foreheads touched.

"How did this happen?" I gasped. "How could I let him do this?"

Max came around the other side of me and put his arm over Sarah's so that they held me up between them.

I struggled for air. "I can't believe I've been so . . . How could I . . . How could he?"

"Exactly," Sarah said. "How could he? It was wrong before, but now that I know how long it has been going on, Cyrus's abuse is downright heinous."

"Twelve years." She wasn't asking for an account, but all at once I wanted to lay it all bare. "Cyrus has been abusing me for twelve years. It's mostly verbal abuse. Emotional, I suppose. But he hits me sometimes, too. He's bigger than me, stronger, and when he's upset about something . . . He's like a kid who doesn't know his own strength."

"He knows his own strength," Max said. "He's perfectly capable of controlling himself in every other life situation. The fact that he loses it with you does not exonerate him of wrongdoing."

I put my hands to my mouth, holding in tears or more damning words, I didn't know. But I did know that something irrevocable had happened: They knew. Max and Sarah knew exactly who Cyrus was. What he had done. I couldn't take that back. I couldn't pretend that the wounds he had inflicted were the result of my own clumsiness anymore. Every time my skin blossomed beneath a bruise, they would take one look at me and know.

It was a frightening thought. But freeing, too. I wasn't alone anymore. And like a bird who has been caged for too long, I watched almost fearfully as the door to my prison creaked open. I didn't know if I had the courage to fly away.

The days after Max and Sarah comforted me in the back of Eden were some of the most conflicted of my life. Lily was still giving me the silent treatment, and I couldn't bring myself to call up Max or Sarah, even if that was the most logical course of action. I was so ashamed. They knew me, they knew the dirty secret of my messy life, and in the light of their understanding I felt filthy and dark.

Complicating everything was the fact that Cyrus was unusually quiet. Our house echoed with an uneasy hush. Sometimes, over the scrape and clatter of knives and forks at mealtimes, I would chance a peek at my tight-lipped husband only to find him staring at me. He'd smile thinly at me over the dish of green beans, and though it seemed an innocent, even friendly gesture, his eyes were cold.

I half expected Cyrus to confront me. Surely his icy calculation could only mean one thing—he knew. But I kept up appearances and tried to explain away any strangeness on my part by citing the upcoming holiday.

Thanksgiving was a big day for the Price family, and all of the work fell to me. Cyrus's mom flew in from Atlanta with her new husband, and extended relatives came from all over the United States to congregate in the tiny town where they had all originated. Cyrus and I hosted a giant feast that could have been featured in the pages of *Better Homes and Gardens.*

Although everything was picture perfect, Thanksgiving was always an awkward afternoon complete with embarrassing displays of family dysfunction. But the Price family was nothing if not proper, and we all politely looked the other way when Uncle Theodore drank too much or Aunt Rose complained about how hard it was to find good help these days. Cyrus even tolerated his arrogant stepdad, Walt, without resorting to shouting or name calling. Of course, he was helped along by generous amounts of single-malt scotch.

When everyone started arriving on Thanksgiving afternoon, I was knotted so tightly I was convinced you could practically see the tension radiate off me. Cyrus welcomed our guests with an unusual expansiveness, a forced benevolence that made me more nervous than if he had scowled and hidden in his study. But I tied a neat bow in my designer apron strings and twisted my lips into a semblance of a smile. If I could make it through a Price family holiday, I could make it through anything.

"Hello, Diana," I said, bussing my mother-in-law's cheek as she swept into the kitchen. She studied my sparkling counters with a critical eye, then plucked a carrot spear from the platter of crudités I had set out. After sniffing it delicately, she took a tiny bite.

"I hope your turkey is organic." Diana's voice was whisper-smooth but it carried a blunt edge. "Walt is on a special diet."

"You should have told me," I said. "I could have customized the menu to fit his needs."

"Too late now." Diana breezed out of the kitchen, but not before she gave me a pointed look. There was no way I could have known about Walt's new diet, but her meaning was unmistakable: You should have asked.

Everyone else arrived with similar expectations and feelings of entitlement. Aunt Rose was put out that the weather was crummy. Uncle Theodore was unimpressed by Cyrus's selection of scotch. Even Lily was petulant. I had made three kinds of pie for dessert, but not her favorite, raisin cream.

"Sweetheart, no one eats it but you," I told her when she realized that there was apple, pumpkin, and pecan, but no raisin cream. "I'll make you your very own pie next week. You can eat the whole thing."

"Whatever," she huffed and stormed to her room.

I had carefully penned place cards, but when everyone took their seats before the Thanksgiving feast it quickly became obvious that no one had liked my arrangement. Cyrus's family had swapped cards and sat wherever they wanted, and I ended up sandwiched between my fractious mother-in-law and my brooding husband. As I slipped into my chair I shot up a prayer for patience.

Cyrus read from the Bible, but I wasn't paying much attention. The sound of scripture as it rolled off his tongue often carried a metallic clang. It seemed harsh and judgmental, not at all like the love story that Max and Sarah tried to convince me it was. I had grown up in a culture steeped in rules and regulations, swift punishment and rigorous standards. Cyrus's God was an exacting taskmaster and one that I had grown to distrust.

At the end of Cyrus's long-winded prayer, everyone said, "Amen." Then the dishes were ceremoniously passed. It started with the heaped platter of turkey and progressed from stuffing to mashed potatoes to homemade cranberry sauce. There were gravy boats on either end of the table and an assortment of salads that were mostly ignored. My sweet potatoes were legendary, and I tried not to roll my eyes as I watched Walt scrape off the brown sugar and pecan topping, forsaking the creamy potatoes beneath. I was quite sure the calorie-rich crumble didn't meet the restrictions of his diet. But I smiled politely and held my tongue.

Conversation was sporadic and littered with gossip. Everyone from out of town wanted to know the local buzz, and Diana regaled us with salacious stories of her social circles in Atlanta that sounded a lot like the plot of a reality TV show. I tried to tune it all out and even managed to catch Lily's eye once and dart her a furtive wink. She ignored me.

Because I wasn't paying attention to the tedious banter, I didn't hear Diana's complaint until she had already voiced it twice. Suddenly the entire table had turned their attention to me, and I found myself looking up from my plate as if I was coming out of a trance. "Pardon me?"

Diana sighed. "I was just saying that your potatoes are pasty. Did you boil them too long?"

I had a forkful of potatoes poised in midair and I slowly lowered it to my plate. "I suppose so," I said. "Sorry about that."

"If there's one thing I can't stand, it's pasty potatoes." Diana gave an affected little shudder and shoved the remains of her gravy-soaked potatoes to the very edge of her plate with the tines of her fork.

"Sorry, Mom." Cyrus looked past me and gave his mother a sympathetic smile. "Rachel's not exactly the world's best cook."

Diana laughed and put a slender hand over her heart as if that was the funniest thing she had ever heard. "Honestly, honey," she said, addressing me, "I don't know what you do all day long. If I were you I'd at least master the art of making decent mashed potatoes."

There were chuckles around the table, and I tried to muster up a sheepish grin so that they knew I was laughing with them. Cyrus's family loved nothing more than to remind me of my humble roots, and in light of some of the other insults I had endured in the past—being called everything from white trash to the daughter of a worthless nail bender—complaining about my potatoes was nothing. Usually I had the grace to bear it. But the events of the past few weeks had brewed together to create the perfect storm, the sort of emotional chaos inside me that was one snide comment away from unleashing destruction. I felt my hands begin to tremble, and I pushed my chair back so I could escape for a moment to refresh the water pitcher. A few minutes alone would do much to fortify my patience.

I was on my feet when Lily spoke up. Her voice cut through the murmurs of amusement, and it was razor sharp. Hard as steel. "My mother is an amazing cook."

Diana's smile withered on her lips and fell away. Lily was her only grandchild, and though Diana could not be considered loving, she had a certain proprietary affection for her granddaughter. They enjoyed a polite relationship that consisted mostly of expensive gifts and the occasional light, ladylike chat.

"I was only teasing her, Lillian Grace." Diana fluffed her platinum coif with the palm of her hand and sniffed. "You don't have to take things so seriously."

I ducked my head to hide the glint in my eye. No one stood up to Diana, and while a part of me wished that Lily had just left well enough alone, it was hugely entertaining to see my mother-in-law so frazzled. In my mind I gave Lily a quick squeeze, then I reached for the water pitcher as if nothing had happened.

But Lily wasn't finished. "It's mean," she huffed. "I hate it when you do that."

My eyes flew to Diana. She was staring at Lily, her jaw uncharacteristically slack. "Excuse me?" She turned to Cyrus. "Did your daughter just call me mean?"

"Of course not." Cyrus gave Lily a hard look. "Did you?"

I could tell just by glancing at my daughter that this thing was not going to blow over. She had moped in silence for weeks, but I should have known that it was just a matter of time before everything came bubbling to the surface. We had covered a lot of ground in the two short months that I worked for Max, and Lily's polished life had taken on a very different sheen. I had hoped that we could deal with it slowly, over time. But it looked as if all her angst was going to come out in the worst possible place: over the Thanksgiving table.

"Lily," I cut in quickly, "I need your help in the kitchen. Come with me, please."

"No," Lily and Cyrus said at exactly the same time.

"She needs to apologize to her grandmother," Cyrus said, shushing Lily with a raised hand.

"I will not apologize." Lily crossed her arms over her chest and gave the entire table her most belligerent glare. "It's horrible the way you all belittle Mom. I hate it. *You* need to apologize to *her*."

My heart turned to stone in my chest. "No, Lily," I said. "It's fine. They're just teasing."

"No, they're not." Lily turned her focus to me and I was surprised to see the depth of emotion in her eyes. She was desperate to be heard, to be understood. "I just want everyone to see you the way that I do. You're so beautiful, Mom. So good at what you do . . . so talented . . ."

Cyrus snorted. "Not at mashing potatoes," he said snidely.

The rest of the table relaxed: We were back in familiar territory. They thought one cutting attempt at humor would put this all to rest. But even as they went back to their turkey, I could see that Lily was downright furious. I hurried around the table and put my hands on her shoulders, willing her to keep her mouth shut with the press of my fingers. "I need your help," I told her again. "Let's go."

"Mom is very talented," Lily hissed as I half dragged her out of her seat. "She could run a catering business. Or start a bakery." Lily's eyes went wide and she stabbed a finger into the air triumphantly. "Better yet, she could open her own tailor shop now that Mr. Wever is going out of business. Did you know that just one of her suits is worth two thousand dollars? *Two thousand dollars.*"

Lily came abruptly to her senses as a hush descended over the table. She gave a little gasp, but after that harsh sound the room fell so flat you could practically hear each individual heartbeat. I squeezed my eyes shut, but I could still feel the heat of shock as everyone turned their attention to me. I should have said something witty, tried to deflect the weight of all that was coming, but I was too numb to respond.

"Mr. Wever? You mean that immigrant seamstress?" Cyrus said, his tone light. I hadn't noticed that he had come out of his chair, and when he put his arm around my waist I was so startled I jumped. He tightened his grip, pulling me toward him as he whispered, "Max Wever ... Now that's a name I haven't heard in a very long time."

CHAPTER 15

MITCH

December 24, 5:00 P.M.

Mitch isn't hungry, so the nurse's aide brings him dinner in his room where he can nibble at his leisure. The tray is deceptively grand, a trio of plates topped with elegant chrome food covers that reflect Mitch's face back to him in distorted caricatures like the trick mirrors in a fun house. He studies himself from various angles before peeking at the meal that lies beneath, but after a feast of pancakes, blueberry sauce, and sausage in the morning, the evening meal is uninspiring. Lukewarm chicken a la king and green beans that look like lengths of plastic tubing.

The only thing Mitch eats is dessert. One of those poke cakes with red and green jello swirled through the white and an inch of whipped cream on top. There is a mini candy cane on the plate beside the cake, and although he doesn't like candy canes, he loves the smell. Mitch takes the plastic wrapper off so that he can sniff the peppermint.

Scents are a powerful trigger, Mitch decides, because breathing in the sharp, bright fragrance stirs up a hundred different memories. They flit around his mind like confetti in one of those fancy snow globes, and though he cannot single one out and examine it, Mitch is happy for just a moment to enjoy the feeling of warmth the candy cane evokes. Somewhere, deep inside, everything is still there. It's just hidden away.

Mitch takes one last sniff of the candy cane, then deposits it on his dessert plate. He carries the lunchroom tray to the small table just inside his door and shuffles back to the rocking chair in his slippers. There's a photograph of a little girl on the windowsill, and a pretty paper ornament hanging from the latch. It sparkles in the light from his lamp. But Mitch doesn't pay much attention to either of these things. Instead, he reaches for the tattered notebook that rests on the seat of the chair. He picks it up and eases into the worn cushions with a sigh.

There are a thousand things he does not remember, but this notebook fits the contours of his hands. He has held it so many times the blue cardboard cover has faded to a milky white in places, and the edges of the papers are rolled and frayed. But in spite of the fact that it has been heavily used, Mitch always anticipates opening the cover with an almost childlike excitement. No matter how many times he has read the pages, Mitch does not remember what is written inside.

His mouth curves in a bittersweet smile as he lifts the cover and pushes down a wave of anticipation that is tinged with sadness. It's a diary of sorts. No, a book of letters. There is a date scribbled in one corner, and, glancing at the calendar that hangs over his bed, Mitch realizes that the words were penned seven years earlier. Seven years. It's a long time. A lifetime.

He begins to read.

Dear Rachel,

Where to begin? You know firsthand that I've never been good with words, and now the doctors tell me I'm only going to get worse. I can't put this off much longer. If I do, I won't have anything left to say at all.

The diagnosis is Alzheimer's. After my stroke I started to forget things, and now they tell me that the wires in my brain are getting tangled. Can you imagine? Tangles in my brain. Like when you were little and I combed your hair on Sunday mornings. Once there was a knot that was so snarled I had to cut it out with a scissors. Do you remember that? I guess it wouldn't work to cut out the tangles in my head.

I wish we could have those days back. Those years when you were small and needed help combing your hair. I tried to be gentle, but I know you sometimes cried. I'm so sorry for that. There are a lot of things that I would change if I could.

Like the last time we spoke. I was so angry. But even more than that, I was afraid. I know who Cyrus is, Rachel. I spent fifteen years with an abuser, and I can spot them from a mile away. I could tell from the very first time I laid eyes on Cyrus Price that he was going to hurt you. I would have done anything to stop that from happening, but instead of pushing you away from him, I pushed you away from myself. And now, I want you to know that I'm going to finally let you go. Maybe if I stop chasing you, you'll turn around and see that I've been waiting here all along.

I'm not very good at this, am I? I told you I wasn't. Maybe if I was better at expressing myself, we wouldn't be in this position. How many years has it been since I've seen you? Five? More? I lose track of time here, but it feels like forever. I would give anything to talk face to face.

It's probably too little, too late, but I'm going to tell you everything I remember. Why I loved your mother. Why I wanted to protect her. How I spent most of my life believing that love and provision were the same thing. That if I kept *you sheltered and clothed and fed, you'd be fine. I know now that while I worked my fingers to the bone, all you wanted was my attention. My time. Maybe if I had worked less and held you more everything would be different.*

Sometimes I dream that I am young again. You are small. Freckle-faced and cute as can be. It makes my heart ache to remember you like that. And you know what? In my sleep I do things differently. I listen when you talk. I leave work early. I stop your mother when she says those horrible things to you. I tell her that she's dead wrong. That you're perfect.

I always wake up from those dreams feeling lost. I don't remember who I am or how I managed to mess things up so bad. I'd give anything to go back. To make those dreams come true.

Do you know that I used to watch you sleep? I had to be on the job site before dawn, but every morning before I left I would go into your room. It was the best five minutes of my day. I loved the moonlight on your face. The way you slept with your cheek in your hand. You looked so peaceful I could believe that everything was right in the world.

I prayed over you every morning. And God must have heard my prayers because in spite of everything you grew in grace and beauty every single day. You are precious, my darling Rachel. You are my angel.

> *Love,*
> *Daddy*

CHAPTER 16

RACHEL

November 24–December 24

I told the doctor I had slipped in the bathroom and it wasn't a word of a lie. Of course, I didn't include the small detail that Cyrus had contributed to my fall, but Dr. Sutton wouldn't have believed me even if I dared to spill the whole, unvarnished truth. By the time the good doctor was casting my wrist, Cyrus had transformed into the perfect, doting husband. He held my uninjured hand throughout the entire procedure, and even went so far as to brush my forehead with the occasional kiss. It was almost more than I could bear. But not because Cyrus was being duplicitous. Because he was being sincere.

After Lily blurted my secret to his entire family, Cyrus managed to hold his temper in check until everyone had enjoyed their pie and coffee. Then, when the final car pulled away from the curb, he marched to our bedroom without a backward glance. He wouldn't challenge me in front of Lily, but I knew from experience what awaited me when she went to bed.

"Let's go," Lily whispered to me, even though Cyrus was an entire floor away.

"What do you mean?"

"Let's get out of here." There was an edge of desperation in her voice. "Hop in the car and just drive."

"Are you kidding?" I put the final saucer in the dishwasher and added a swig of liquid detergent. "Where in the world would we go?"

"I don't know. Somewhere. Anywhere. Let's go find grandpa!" Lily caught me by the elbow and squeezed.

"Sweetheart, please." My heart was stuttering at her mention of my father, but the hope I felt was quick and baseless. Instead of responding, I turned around and drew her to me, wrapping my arms around her slender shoulders. "It's fine. Everything is going to be just fine."

"But I told Dad about Mr. Wever!"

I smoothed her hair absently, a little stunned that the numbness that had settled over me at her Thanksgiving dinner proclamation had not yet gone away. Maybe I should have been scared, but I felt anesthetized. All I could think was: *So, it's come to this.* I didn't even know what this was.

"What's the worst that could happen?" I asked. It was a rhetorical question, and when Lily didn't respond I pressed my cheek to the top of her head and wished her a good night's sleep.

"I can't just go to bed," she argued. There were tears threatening in her eyes, but I ignored them. I didn't have the wherewithal to comfort her, no matter how much I wanted to.

"You don't have a choice." I took her by the hand and led her to her room. I would have locked her inside if I could. Instead, I closed the door behind me and prayed that an angel would stand guard.

From there, the night progressed rather predictably except for one thing: I was not the same cowering maiden I had always been. Cyrus was furious, but instead of dodging his verbal attack I met it head-on. I took a deep breath and faced it. I didn't deny the truth or try to sugarcoat the fact that I had lied to him for weeks. Instead, as my husband got increasingly angry, I remained calm. And even though I was trembling inside, I could feel that there was something different in the way I held my tongue. Usually my silence was born of fear and shame, but as Cyrus worked himself into a lather, I realized that my self-possession was the result of a flickering inner peace. I had a long way to go, but I could see the woman that I wanted to be. She was within reach.

Unfortunately, the more tranquil I appeared, the more livid Cyrus became. When he finally flung me across the master bathroom, I was only surprised that he had managed to control himself for so long. As I crouched on the tile floor, I knew that my wrist was broken. But it hardly seemed to matter. I had eyes only for Cyrus, and the expression he wore was one that I had not seen in a very long time. My husband was sorry for what he had done.

In the beginning of our marriage, Cyrus was always repentant when he raised a hand to me. But as the years progressed, it was almost as if I could watch him fall out of love with me. It happened a degree at a time, until one day Cyrus shoved me out of his way and didn't look back when I fell. Even though I was physically fine, that one push hurt more than if he had pummeled me with his fists. It seemed to mark the moment that our relationship died.

All that changed in the bathroom on Thanksgiving night. Before I could even cry out in pain, Cyrus was on his knees beside me. He didn't apologize, but he lifted me carefully to my feet and guided me downstairs. When I was settled in the car, he went to check on Lily, then rushed me to the emergency room, where he acted like it was pure agony to watch me suffer.

I believed him.

A part of me was dying to ask Cyrus why he could suddenly look on me with tenderness. But a much larger part was content to bask in the longed-for attention, to smile shyly and keep my mouth shut. Maybe my newfound confidence had changed me in my husband's eyes. Maybe this was a new beginning.

Although Cyrus and I never talked about what happened, in the weeks after the Thanksgiving fiasco we enjoyed a tenuous peace. I was brave in ways that I had never been before, inviting Sarah over for coffee a few afternoons, and even serving homemade pizzas at the granite island in the kitchen one night. Cyrus looked a little taken aback by the casual meal—it was a far cry from our customarily grand suppers around the dining room table—but he didn't complain.

The only thing that I did not have the confidence to do was mention Max in any way. I missed his company, especially with Christmas approaching, but things were going so well between Cyrus and me that I couldn't bring myself to broach the topic of my forbidden relationship. What if I dredged up all of our old bitterness? The mere thought of reverting to where we had been made my heart wring inside my chest.

"I don't get it," Lily said one afternoon as we were

curled up on the couch. It was the first day of her Christmas vacation and we were watching *The Sound of Music*, a tradition we had started when she was in kindergarten.

"What don't you get?" I asked absently, reaching for another handful of popcorn. I smiled to myself as I tossed a few kernels in my mouth. Popcorn on the couch on a Wednesday afternoon? It was unheard of in the Price house.

"I don't get what happened between you and Dad."

I pursed my lips for a moment, trying to think of a way to explain. Eventually, I gave up. "I don't get it either!" I laughed. "But I'm not going to overanalyze it. I'm happy, Lil. Things are good."

Lily cocked her head a little as she studied me. "You're happy?" she asked.

"I am."

"But I don't think things are good."

I shifted on the couch and gave her my full attention. "What are you talking about? Things haven't been this . . ." I cast around for the right word, "untroubled in years. Look at us! Your dad will be home in twenty minutes and I haven't even started supper. Granted, we're having stir-fry and I have to do it last minute, but still."

Lily looked pointedly at my wrist.

"It was an accident," I sighed.

"No, it wasn't."

"Well, that was before. This is after."

"What about Mr. Wever?" Lily crossed her arms over her chest.

"What about Mr. Wever?"

"Why can't I go visit him? It's almost Christmas; he shouldn't be alone."

I plucked at a frayed end of the afghan we had spread over our laps. "Max is a touchy subject," I said. "I'm not sure that I'm ready to bring him up just yet."

"What about grandpa? Maybe if we can't see Max we could—"

"Lily, stop. We can't track down your grandpa."

"Why not?"

"Because—"

"Then nothing's changed," Lily interrupted. "This house is still full of rules I don't understand. Things we can't say and things that we're supposed to say . . . I don't get it. I don't want to live like this anymore."

"I have a feeling we're on the verge of something new," I said, weaving my fingers through Lily's. "Something new and good."

She crinkled her nose doubtfully. "I sure hope so."

I should have known that when something seems too good to be true, it usually is. A few nights after I assured Lily that our lives were about to be made new, I forgot a load of Cyrus's dress shirts in the washing machine. My Bible study had decided to deliver Christmas goodies to the local nursing home, and instead of keeping up with the laundry I abandoned a load in the middle of a cycle. What can I say? It completely slipped my mind.

When Sarah told me we were headed to the manor, something inside my chest collapsed. My father had been relocated to a care facility years ago, but the Everton home was too expensive and he had been forced to leave. The scant information I gathered about my dad's whereabouts came via infrequent updates from my uncle, but even those brief messages had stopped a few years back. Suddenly, the mere thought of visiting a nursing home had me in knots.

My father was out there somewhere. Was he lonely? Did he think of me? What would he say if he knew that Lily wanted to see him? That she harbored a quiet longing to meet the man who shared her blood?

As I walked the halls of the care home, passing out decorative tins filled with shortbread cookies and walnut fudge, I caught myself looking for my dad in the face of every resident. I was leveled by my own response, the almost frantic way I searched their features for something familiar. It had been a very long time since I thought of my father with anything but indifference, but the weeks of recounting my childhood for Lily had opened up a secret corner in my soul—a place I had worked hard to forget.

I wanted to see my dad. It was a shocking realization, and as we pulled away from the care home I found myself sobbing in the passenger seat of Sarah's car.

"I think I miss him," I confessed when Sarah pulled over and handed me a tissue. "I don't know why ... I mean, things were never very good between us."

"He's your father," Sarah said gently. "Nothing can change that."

"But we haven't spoken for years." I tried to blow my nose discreetly. "I can't imagine why this is hitting me so hard right now."

"It's been a life-changing couple of months," Sarah said with a gentle laugh. "You rekindled a decades-old friend-ship, lied to your husband, came clean with your daughter, spent hours recounting your past, had a massive blowout with Cyrus, and ... finally reconciled?" Her voice tweaked upward at the mention of reconciliation. It hit me that my friend was as dubious about my happily-ever-after ending as my daughter was.

"Yes," I said firmly. Then, with less conviction, "I don't know. Things have been better between me and Cyrus, but it's not like we suddenly have a fabulous marriage."

Sarah looked like she wanted to press me further, but a fresh tear slid down my cheek and she seemed to think better of it. Patting my hand, she said, "Well, I for one totally understand why you would like to see your father after all this time. Your whole life has been one big upheaval lately and there's nothing quite like a hug from your daddy to make the world seem sane again."

Even though I could hardly remember what a hug from my daddy felt like, I gave a little nod.

"So," Sarah shrugged. "Go see him."

"It's not that easy. I don't even know where he is."

Sarah's eyes sparkled. "Ooh. A mystery. I love a good mystery."

She dropped me off at home with a squeeze and a promise that we would track down my dad. It couldn't be too hard, right?

My head was spinning with memories of the past and hopes for the future when I kicked off my boots that afternoon. I hung my coat in the entryway and left my gloves neatly folded on the hall table beside my keys, then I wandered into the kitchen where I began absently searching the fridge for something to fix for supper. By the time Lily got home from school I was busy rolling out the pastry for my famous beef Wellington, and the load of laundry that I had abandoned in the washing machine had been totally and completely forgotten.

Until the next morning when Cyrus got up for work.

I had just cracked two eggs into a hot frying pan when Cyrus stormed into the kitchen bare-chested and visibly upset. His skin was pink from the scalding water of his shower and his hair was still damp.

"Where is my blue striped shirt?" he demanded.

There was a vein bulging in his forehead, and I could feel the anger radiating off him. "Uh," I faltered, trying to remember why his favorite shirt wasn't hanging in his closet where it always was. It hit me in a rush. "In the washing machine," I said, my stomach sinking. "We went to the nursing home yesterday, and I guess I never moved the load of colors to the dryer."

"My shirt is in the washing machine?" Cyrus looked incredulous. "It's the annual chamber Christmas brunch this morning. What am I supposed to wear?"

A drop of butter spurted from the hot pan and burned a pinprick spot on the back of my hand. My attention was drawn to the sizzling eggs. If I let them go much longer the yolks would be hard. Cyrus hated hard yolks. "I'm so sorry," I said, reaching for the spatula. "I didn't mean to—"

"Don't turn your back on me!"

I jumped a little when Cyrus yelled, dropping the spatula into the pan. One of the yolks spilled yellow across the teflon surface. My perfect morning eggs were ruined. "It was an accident," I said, pulling the pan off the stove, trying to explain. "My Bible study went to the nursing home, and it got me thinking about my dad . . ."

"What's your dad got to do with this?"

"Nothing," I blurted, surprised by the venom in Cyrus's tone. I had been planning to broach the topic of my dad over breakfast, but apparently that wasn't a wise move. "I'm just trying to explain why I forgot about the shirt."

"I don't need excuses. I need my shirt."

"Can't you wear another one?" I asked timidly.

"Can't you have my laundry done when I need it?" Cyrus took a step closer to me and I backed up against the stove. "Seriously, Rachel. Is it so hard to get a load of laundry done? What do you do all day? I know you snuck around with Max for a few weeks, but I thought you got that out of your system."

"You make it sound so dirty," I whispered, shrinking into myself so that there was less of me for Cyrus to hate. "Max is my friend."

"Your friend? You think a man who would encourage you to defy your husband is a friend?"

I closed my eyes for a second and berated myself for being so blind. So stupid. Of course, it was all coming out. Cyrus wasn't the type to let anything slide, much less the sort of offense that I had perpetrated against him. Against our marriage. I knew the rules and I had directly disobeyed them. Did I really think I would get off scot free?

"I thought you had forgiven me for that." I didn't even realize I had spoken out loud until Cyrus gave a short, dry laugh.

"You never asked for forgiveness," he sneered.

It didn't seem the right time to mention that I believed that was the point of real forgiveness: It was freely given. Grace-filled. Unsolicited. Instead, it seemed the right time to edge away. To slip slowly from the room and try to find another shirt that my husband would find suitable for brunch with the Everton bigwigs. It was a shirt, for heaven's sake. But I knew that Cyrus's anger stemmed from somewhere much deeper. Somewhere that seethed with resentment over the years that had built up between us. The various and sundry ways that he was sure I had failed him.

"I really am sorry," I said, reverting to survival mode. Maybe if I seemed repentant enough, Cyrus would calm down and remember that we were on the verge of patching things up. Hadn't he looked at me with something akin to compassion only nights before? Of course, compassion was a far cry from love, but it was a start. I could still feel the warm graze of his lips against my forehead. Had that really happened? Or had I imagined it?

"Sorry isn't good enough, Rach." Cyrus caught my wrist and squeezed too tight for comfort. "I don't ask for much, but there are a few things that I do require. I can't believe that after all this time you would let yourself be so lazy. Do you have any idea how hard I work for us? What it takes to keep a house like this up and running?"

I shook my head, afraid to meet his gaze. Somewhere, cowering deep inside, was the woman who had felt so confident only a day before. But she was terrified now, reminded of her position in this family and her own worthlessness. She was scared and ashamed, and she didn't even flinch when Cyrus hit her.

"Good morning," Lily muttered when she shuffled into the kitchen that morning. I couldn't tell if she was being facetious or not, but she eyed the bruise that was beginning to color my cheekbone with an air of consternation. "Mom!"

"Oh, it's fine." I gave the pancake batter an extra stir and forced a smile. "I'm just so clumsy—"

"Stop it." Lily slapped the counter with her open palm. "Stop lying to me. I know the truth. You've told me everything."

Not everything, I thought, but I held my tongue. "How about some blueberry pancakes?" I asked cheerfully.

"No thanks." Lily turned away and headed toward the stairs.

"But you have to have something to eat," I called after her.

"I'm not hungry."

"But—"

"I said, I'm not hungry."

I watched her until her stocking feet disappeared on the carpeted landing of the second floor. When her door slammed, I jumped a little and left a splat of pancake batter on the counter. How could things have changed so quickly? Our all-too-briefly happy home was once again a battleground. And the change had quite literally happened overnight. I didn't know whether to laugh or cry.

For the next couple of days, the air in our house was brittle with things unsaid. Lily spent long hours in her pajamas and kept to herself as much as she could, and Cyrus worked extra shifts even though he usually took time off around the holidays. I think they were both avoiding me, and the visible reminder that graced my cheek of how bitter our lives had become.

None of that changed the fact that it was almost Christmas. That our ten-foot artificial tree sparkled like a jewel in the living room or that carols wafted from the radio no matter which station I tuned it to. There was a decidedly festive spirit in the air, and in many ways that only made everything worse. The magic of Christmas was completely lost on me this year, and while I should have been contemplating a miracle in a manger, all I could think about was my own gloomy situation.

I was feeling so blue that I entirely forgot about Lily's acting debut until she descended the stairs on the afternoon of Christmas Eve. She was wearing a costume of pearl white that fell in long, overlapping layers and pooled softly around her ankles. There was a creamy swath of faux fur at her collar and along the hem, and a matching muff to tuck her hands in. She was a vision.

"You look amazing," I breathed.

"You forgot about the pageant, didn't you?" Lily screwed up the corner of her mouth.

I sighed a little. "I suppose I did. But that doesn't mean I'm not proud of you. It doesn't mean I'm not excited to see you play the part of an angel."

"I don't feel like doing it anymore." Lily swept across the floor and flounced on the couch with a huff. "I'm not in the mood."

"Oh, honey." I crossed the room and perched on the arm of the couch, trailing my fingers through her auburn hair. "I know the last few days have been hard. But we can't lose sight of what this season is all about."

"If you're so excited about it, why don't you be the angel?"

"Are you kidding me? Look at you!" I took an inch of the silky fabric between my thumb and forefinger and gave it an appreciative rub. "You're breathtaking."

"There are wings, too," Lily said, trying to sound indifferent, but a sliver of excitement crept into her voice all the same.

"Well then, I guess all we have to do is your hair."

She gave me a skeptical look. "What could we do?"

"Something elaborate." I gathered her curls in my hands and swept them up on the top of her head. "I'll do a few loose braids, and then pin it all up with little pieces hanging down."

"Sounds pretty."

"It'll be gorgeous."

"But your arm. . . ?" she gave my casted wrist a look of severe disapproval.

"My fingers still work. See?" I waggled my fingers to show her that my hand wasn't completely useless, and raised my eyebrows hopefully.

Lily lifted one shoulder in a shrug of nonchalance, but I could tell she wanted to be won over. "If you want to mess around with it, you can. We'll see if it turns out."

"Just let me grab a few things." I scooted out of the room and was back before Lily had time to change her mind again. Fixing her hair was a definite bright spot in a week that felt as dark and dreary as the weather outside.

"It's supposed to storm tonight," I told her as my fingers struggled to work elegant braids in her red-gold hair. "I hope it's not snowing too hard for the program."

" 'The show must go on,' " Lily intoned. "At least, that's what Sarah says. She told us that the snow will only add to the drama."

"I can hear her saying that." I laughed a little, and was seized by a sudden desire to see my friend. I hadn't seen her since our afternoon at the nursing home, and I wondered if she was busy trying to track down my father. I imagined Sarah was an intrepid sleuth, but I didn't know how to break it to her that even if she discovered where my dad was staying, it wouldn't matter anymore. Cyrus would never let me go.

It didn't take me long to make Lily look like she had fallen from heaven, but I lingered over her hair for a few stolen minutes. I could tell that she was still upset by the way she held her shoulders, but at least we were occupying the same space. It felt good to be near her.

When the garage door slammed, my heart sank to my toes. The afternoon had slipped away from me, and it was nearly five o'clock. Time to drop Lily off at the farm for last-minute preparations before the big Christmas pageant at six. Almost time to make my public debut, bruised face and all. I wasn't cheered by the thought. Over the years I had grown to hate showcasing the evidence of my failed love. I hated the looks people shot me. The lies I had to tell.

I heaved a sigh and gathered up the hair things just as Cyrus was walking into the living room. "What's she all dressed up for?" he demanded, looking from me to Lily and back again as if he suspected we were up to something.

"She's the angel for the Christmas program," I said. I resisted the urge to roll my eyes—we had been over this a half dozen times. "I'm just going to put this stuff away and then I'll bring her to the farm."

Cyrus gaped at me. "Oh, no, you won't."

"Pardon me?" I paused midstep and tried not to appear as frustrated as I felt.

"You will not bring Lily to the farm looking like that."

I glanced down at my clothes and found nothing offensive in the tailored jeans and fitted jacket I had on. One hand reached absently for my hair and I pulled a soft strand over my shoulder, wondering if I had messed it up somehow. "I'll change," I said. "I wasn't planning on wearing a dress because it's supposed to be cold, but maybe if I wear boots . . ."

"I'm not talking about your clothes." Cyrus had been unbuttoning his coat, but now he redid the last few buttons and motioned to Lily. "Let's go. I'll drop you off."

"No," she said. Her chin was raised, but there was a waver in her voice. "I want Mom to bring me."

"She's not going out of the house like that," Cyrus said as if I wasn't even there.

"Like what?" I asked softly.

"All banged up like that."

My fingers found my cheek, the place where the skin was still tight and smooth as a piece of purple silk pulled taut. "I fell," I said, the words a reflex.

"Well, you look terrible." He turned away from me and barked an order at Lily: "Let's go."

I didn't even realize that Lily was standing until she linked her arm with mine and held on tight. "I'm not going with you," she told Cyrus.

He stopped. "What did you say?" He cast a dark look over his shoulder at Lily, but didn't even bother to face her full on. It was like he couldn't quite bring himself to believe that he was being challenged by his usually compliant daughter.

"Go," I whispered to her. "I'll see you when you get back. You're going to make a beautiful angel."

"No," Lily said again, as much for Cyrus as for me. She took a deep breath. "I won't go with him."

"Lillian Grace," Cyrus whirled around and whispered her name through clenched teeth. "Get over here, now. We're leaving."

"No." It was softer this time.

"Sweetie," I took her face in my hands, "just go. Everything is going to be fine. We'll—"

Cyrus cut me off abruptly by swallowing the distance between us in a few giant strides and grabbing Lily by the arm. He didn't normally touch her, and certainly not in a rough way—I had done my best to make sure any anger he felt was always directed at me—and when he jerked Lily away from me she cried out as if she had been struck.

I can't really explain what happened in my chest except to say that somewhere deep inside me a fuse blew. It was a tiny thing, a quiet disconnect that changed everything so entirely I knew in that moment that there was no going back.

"Take your hand off her." I said it so quietly I wondered for a second if Cyrus would even hear me, but something in my tone stopped him cold.

"What did you say?"

"I said, *take your hand off her.*"

Cyrus had seen me happy and sad, hurt and scared, but I wondered if he had ever seen me blood-boiling furious. I had spent a good chunk of my life trying to hide my true self from my husband, trying to mold myself to the woman he wanted me to be so that there would never be a reason for him to be angry. But all of that striving fell away the second Lily cried out. Something wild burst inside me and all at once I knew that if he wanted to get to my daughter, he'd have to go through me first.

Enraged, I took a quick step forward and wrenched Lily's arm free from Cyrus's grip. Shoving her behind me, I glared at my husband. "If you ever lay a hand on her again, I'll . . ."

"What?" Cyrus looked stunned at my defiance, but he managed to pull his lips into a sneer all the same. "What do you think you're going to do, Rachel? You think you can hurt me?"

"I don't want to hurt you," I choked. "But I won't let you hurt her."

"Mom?" Lily gripped the back of my jacket with desperate fingers. I could tell by the little gasps of her ragged breathing that she was crying.

"It's okay," I told her. I didn't dare to turn my back on Cyrus, but I reached behind me and caught her hand in my own. "We're leaving."

I took a tentative step backward, and Lily followed my lead. We had backed halfway out of the living room and were well on our way to the front door when Cyrus seemed to come to his senses.

"What do you mean you're leaving?" The muscles in his jaw tightened visibly.

"We're leaving," I said again, because the truth was, I didn't know what I meant. All I knew was that Lily and

I had to go, now, and whatever it took to get us out the
door was exactly what I was willing to do.

"It's Christmas Eve, Rachel. What are you going to do?
Run away? You can't even check into a hotel. The credit
cards are in my name."

I faltered. Cyrus was right: I had no idea what I was
going to do. I had no money, nowhere to run. I didn't
want to burden Sarah, and going to Max would only drag
someone I dearly loved into a horrible situation. It seemed
like there was no way out, and yet, I couldn't stay. We
couldn't stay. To back down now would only give Cyrus
more power over us. I couldn't stand that thought.

"Keep going, Lil," I said. "Put your boots on and don't
forget your coat."

When we crossed onto the tile floor of the entryway,
something in Cyrus's eyes shifted. He appeared to understand that we weren't going to stop, and he didn't look
too happy that his wife and daughter were on the verge of
walking out of his life.

"Don't you dare." He glowered at me menacingly, walking toward us as if he had all the time in the world.

I felt a rush of panic then, a frantic, anguished surge of
horror that vibrated to my very fingertips. What have I
done? I wondered, but it was too late to take back what I
had said. I could hear Lily struggling with her coat behind
me, and I silently thanked the Lord that we had not yet

affixed her angel wings. A second later I heard her unlock the front door. It was time.

"Go to the car, Lily," I said. And then I turned my back on Cyrus and ran. I didn't even care about my coat or shoes, but my car keys were on the hall table, and as I lunged for them I heard Cyrus make a low, guttural noise.

"What are you going to do, Rach?" he shouted. "Shoot me?"

Confusion made me stumble. Shoot him? What in the world was he talking about? And then, as I half crashed into the hall table, I remembered. There was a gun in the drawer. And I knew how to use it.

Cyrus was too far behind me to stop me from throwing open the drawer and grabbing the weapon inside. In less than a heartbeat, my mind ran through every possible scenario. I knew where the safety catch was, I knew how to cock the hammer. Would Cyrus stop if I pointed it at him? Would I shoot?

A shiver raced up my spine as I felt him move behind me, and in that moment I yanked open the drawer. The gun was there, but so was something I had completely forgotten about. Sarah's book. Perfect love casts out fear ... I didn't have to read the back cover copy to know what it said, what the book was about. It seemed impossible. There is no such thing as perfect love, my mind hissed. But my heart responded with the memory of Max's smile. Sarah's friendship. Lily's hand in mine. I thought of making snow angels with my dad, and suddenly I knew that all the imperfect love I had ever known was a reflection of the perfect love that I had never had the eyes to see. I had a split second and a choice to make.

"I choose love," I breathed as I shoved the drawer shut and whirled around to face Cyrus.

"Are you going to shoot me, Rachel?" Cyrus snarled, slamming into me and grabbing me by the arms so tightly I felt the circulation immediately stop.

"No," I whispered. I was terrified, scared to death that he'd wrench the drawer open and turn that gun on me, but I sent desperate prayers heavenward and managed to croak out, "But you're going to let me go."

"The hell I am." His breath was hot on my skin, and though I was loath to do so, I made myself look my husband in the eyes.

"I loved you so much," I said, and that one tiny admission unleashed a lifetime of tears I had hidden away. They spilled down my face hot and fast.

Cyrus blinked, momentarily surprised, but he was too angry for something as monumental as a declaration of love to shake him back to his senses. I could feel his grip tighten like a vise.

"Oh, Cyrus," I whispered. I knew he probably wanted to kill me, but Max and Sarah had loved me enough to ensure that he wouldn't. "You're going to let me and Lily go because if you don't Max will tell everyone what you've done."

"What?" Spittle flew from Cyrus's lips as he leaned in even closer.

"He knows. He knows everything. If you so much as touch me, Max will scream it from the rooftops. You'll be ruined, Cyrus, and you know it."

"You think people will believe the word from that old man? I'm Cyrus Price, Rachel. My name is as good as gold around here."

"Sarah knows, too." I bit off the words, my voice trembling. "They both know that Cyrus Price beats his wife. They have pretty convincing proof." Even though my arms were numb, I held up my casted wrist, forcing the evidence of my husband's abuse right in his face.

Cyrus searched my eyes, and he must have seen the truth written there, because the air in the room went absolutely still for the span of a few heartbeats. I didn't even realize I was holding my breath until my chest began to ache.

I could count on one hand the times that I had seen Cyrus speechless in my life, but this one eclipsed them all. My husband let go of me as if I had burned him, as if my very skin was made of fire that he couldn't stand to touch. There was nothing Cyrus loved so much as his own reputation, and though people had probably speculated about the nature of our relationship before, a public airing of his sins would destroy everything he had worked so hard for. Cyrus was a small-town hero, the high school football star, son of the former mayor, a business owner who was destined for glory himself. But if everyone knew who he truly was, what he did to me, there would be no forgiveness. Everton was a tiny town, but it was populated by people with big hearts. I wondered at the fact that it had taken me so long to realize it.

"I'm done," I said quietly.

Cyrus stared at me for a long moment, and I could see a host of emotions warring behind his eyes. He was breathing heavily, and I knew that there was nothing he wanted so much as to grab me about the throat and squeeze, but there was something else there, too. Regret? Could it be?

Before I could begin to unravel the mystery that was my husband, Cyrus spun around and smashed his fist into the wall so hard the pictures in the hallway slid crooked on their nails. I gasped at the hole in the drywall, the bloody mess of my husband's knuckles, but he didn't even spare me a glance. Clutching his fist, Cyrus threw open the front door and left.

It wasn't until he was gone that I realized Lily had collapsed in a heap in the corner. She was sobbing quietly, and when I said her name she looked up and began to wail in earnest. I walked carefully to her on shaky legs and sank to the floor beside my crying angel. I wrapped my arms around her slender frame. Kissed her sweet head, and whispered a prayer for every little girl who had to grow up with broken wings. Myself included.

CHAPTER 17

RACHEL

December 24

We packed quickly. I grabbed two suitcases from the back of my giant walk-in closet and gave one to Lily with the instruction to take only that which she could not live without. She stood for a moment in the middle of the upstairs hall and stared at me with wide, scared eyes. Although she was eleven years old, for a few seconds in the middle of all the chaos Lily looked like a very small child. I longed to sweep her up into my arms and cradle her like I did when she was a baby. But before I could pull her to me, my daughter blinked and the spell was broken. She forced a brave smile and nodded. "We're going to be fine," she said.

My heart lodged in my throat. "Yes, we are."

As I frantically tossed clothes into my own suitcase—struggling with only one good hand and cursing the clumsy bulk of my casted wrist—it struck me that the sum of my life with Cyrus could be reduced to the essentials. I packed as if I were going on a vacation—practical clothes, toiletries, a few pairs of shoes—not as if I was leaving my life behind. There were a couple of photo albums filled with pictures of Lily that I shoved between my wadded-up clothes, and at the last moment I snatched a framed picture of Cyrus and me at our wedding. We looked happy, we really did. I briefly touched the reflection of my own young face, the unsuspecting way I tried to hide a half smile, the adoration in my eyes. Maybe, I thought, adding the gilded frame to the pile of things in my suitcase. Maybe.

For all intents and purposes, the suitcases were Cyrus's. As were my clothes, all of Lily's things, and the almost-new SUV I loaded everything into. But I believed that Cyrus owed us more than we took, and I knew that with the threat of Max and Sarah's intimate knowledge of our home life hanging over his head he wouldn't report the vehicle stolen or anything like that. It was too big a risk.

Though I doubted Cyrus would come after us, I was terrified that he might try to stop us. My pulse pounded a feverish rhythm in my veins as I flew from room to room, grabbing at loose ends—coats and a couple of water bottles and my purse. Lily trailed me absently, until I told her to go get in the car.

When everything was ready, the suitcases hurriedly tossed in the back and all the lights in the house turned off—I couldn't stop myself from performing that one last ritual—I slid into the driver's seat and turned the key in the ignition. It was time to go, but I had no idea where.

"Wait!" Lily said from the passenger's seat. "I forgot something."

"But—"

"I'll be right back!" She slipped out the door before I could stop her.

It felt surreal to be waiting in the cold SUV, my breath turning to mist in the winter air. The smell of exhaust made everything seem stark and real, and I grasped for the first time what I had done. What I was about to do. I battled a wave of hopelessness, of an almost paralyzing fear. Wasn't the life I had always known easier than the one I couldn't begin to imagine? I had no idea what waited for us around the next bend.

"I'm ready," Lily said as she hopped back into her seat. The angel costume was bundled in her arms, wings and all. I hadn't even noticed that she had changed into a pair of jeans and a striped sweater. "But we have to bring this back to Sarah before we go."

I glanced at the dashboard clock and realized that it

was only five-thirty. Had my life fallen apart in just over half an hour? It seemed impossible. "I'm so sorry," I whispered, fighting tears. I realized I was on the verge of total panic. "I'm so, so sorry. You're supposed to be an angel tonight . . ."

"It's okay, Mom." Lily put a steadying hand on my arm, apparently convinced that my desperation had everything to do with her play instead of the fact that we were taking the biggest risk of our lives. "Katie really wanted to be the angel anyway. She'll be so happy that she doesn't have to wear a sheep costume anymore."

Lily was so earnest, I laughed in spite of myself. "You are so perfect. So sweet and selfless and perfect."

"I take after my mom." Lily grinned.

"You don't understand." I shook my head and wove my fingers through hers. Made her look me in the eye. "Lillian Grace, you saved me tonight. You saved us. Do you know that? Do you know what a hero you are?"

"Mom," Lily rolled her eyes and tried to wiggle out of my grip, but I only held on tighter.

"I mean it, Lil. No one else has ever stood up for me. Ever. You've given me the strength to put an end to this."

Lily swallowed hard. "I did that?"

"Yes." I nodded. "You did. You made me feel like I was worth fighting for."

"You are worth fighting for."

"I am?" I didn't mean to sound needy, but after so many years of believing that I was worthless, I was still getting used to the notion that maybe I had bought into a terrible lie. A vicious, suffocating, life-quenching lie.

"You are," Lily said, squeezing my hand. "I'd take a bullet for you."

She was so serious, so gorgeous and wide-eyed and truthful that I couldn't help but grin at her. "I'd take a bullet for you," I said. "But I hope it never comes to that."

"Me, too!" Lily drummed the dashboard, letting a little steam off all the emotion we kept bottled inside. "Come on. Let's get out of here."

It felt good to have somewhere to go, a definite destination in mind. I drove to the farm where the pageant was being held with a sense of determination. One step at a time. And this step made a lot of sense—I was crawling out of my skin with anticipation at the thought of seeing Sarah.

Although the inches of accumulating snow were beginning to dim their glow, dozens of strands of white Christmas lights flickered from the farm, which had been transformed into a prairie Bethlehem. As I crept down the gravel road, I marveled at the sheer number of lights that were wrapped around fenceposts and trees alike. This one little corner of creation sparkled bright and inviting in spite of the growing storm.

The church deacons were dressed in reflective jackets so they could direct the flow of traffic, and people bundled in scarves and hats milled around everywhere. I was grateful for the cloak of night, and for the fact that I did not see Cyrus's truck. Granted, the church pageant was the last place I expected him to run, but my husband was full of surprises.

"They're expecting Lily," Mr. Townsend chirped when I rolled down my window. His smile faltered a little when he saw the mark on my face. "Is everything . . . ?"

"We're fine," I said, giving the elderly deacon a tired smile. "We're actually looking for Sarah. Do you know where she is?"

"Can't miss her." His laugh sounded just the tiniest bit manufactured. I followed his pointing finger to the barn where Sarah was standing on a hay bale trying to dole out last-minute instructions to a group of Sunday school kids in full costume. They wore winter coats beneath their shepherd robes and felt cowhides, and they looked like nothing so much as overgrown Weebles. I suppressed a wry chuckle in spite of the situation.

"Do you mind if I just double park here for a minute? We're not staying."

Mr. Townsend gave me a sober look that seemed far too knowing for my comfort. "I'll watch your car," he said kindly. "Go ahead and leave it running."

"Thank you." I gathered up the bundle of Lily's angel costume and told her to stay in the car. "I'll be right back."

She just nodded.

I jogged across the gravel driveway, weaving through people who would have tried to talk to me if I hadn't worn such a look of resolve. As I approached the hay bale where Sarah stood, she clapped her hands together and grinned, sending the kids scuttling off to hide behind the scenes in the hulking barn turned Bethlehem stable. She smiled after them for a moment, then turned her attention to the crowd. She picked me out almost immediately. Her face changed in an instant.

"Rachel," she said under her breath as she jumped down and hurried over to me. "What's wrong? Where's Lily?"

"It's a long story," I said. "But I'm afraid she can't be the angel tonight." Sarah looked confused as I transferred the beautiful costume to her arms. "I'm so sorry."

"But—"

"We're leaving," I interrupted her, fighting an emotion that I didn't have the time to indulge. The thought of leaving my friend nearly tore my heart in two.

Sarah searched my face before pressing her lips together against the tears that sprang to her eyes. "You finally did it," she whispered, throwing her arms around me, bulky costume and all.

"I suppose so. Though I don't really know what 'it' is."

"It is life, sweetie. Rich, abundant, thrilling life! You've embraced it." Sarah laughed, a quick happy tumble of notes that were musical and bright. "What Cyrus did to you is evil. But it struck me the other day that if you turn evil around, you're left with a pretty clear directive: live. And that's exactly what you're doing. You're going to live, Rachel. Really live."

"I am?"

Sarah ignored me. "There's a passage in John that I love . . ." she trailed off, wrinkling up her nose as she tried to remember. " 'The thief comes only to steal and kill and destroy; I have come that you may have life, and have it to the full.' "

Her words were warm and rich as honey. Life to the full. It sounded like a promise: a promise that I longed to believe, but that was almost too good to be true. Could it be? Could that life be for me?

But before I could ponder her words, Sarah pushed back and held me at arm's length. "You have to go see Max."

"What?"

"Right now. I'll call him and tell him to meet you at the shop."

"At Eden? But why? I'd love to say good-bye to Max, but surely he's not at his shop on Christmas Eve."

"He'll meet you there," Rachel said with conviction. "Listen, I'm not asking you, I'm telling you. Go to Eden."

"Fine," I said shrugging helplessly. "Whatever you say."

A sound like a sob broke loose from deep in Sarah's throat, and she pulled me into another bone-crushing hug. "I pray for you," she said against my hair. "Every day. And I won't stop. You're strong and amazing . . . I just know you're going to come out on the other side of this refined like gold."

I tried to whisper my thanks, but I couldn't speak around the heavy stone in my chest.

"I love you, Rachel. I'm so glad you're my friend."

"Me, too." It was the most I could get out.

We pulled apart then, knowing that this would not be the last time that we saw each other. Not by a long shot. I started making my way back to the car, but when I was a few paces away from Sarah I remembered something and turned back.

"Will you do something for me?" I asked.

"Anything."

"Keep an eye on Cyrus."

Sarah's forehead creased at my unusual request. "I don't understand."

"Someone once told me that everyone deserves to be loved."

She bit her lip and shook her head a bit as if she couldn't quite get her mind around my appeal. After a second she caught my eye. Nodded. "Even the unlovable?" she asked.

"Maybe especially them."

The farm was only a five-minute drive from the Everton city limits, so I didn't expect Max to be there when I pulled up at the back door of Eden Custom Tailoring. But his car was parked sideways in the alley, and the steel door was propped open. Golden light spilled across the deep snow, making the tracks that were left by his boots look like bottomless, shadowy craters.

"I want to come, too," Lily said as I put the SUV in park.

"Of course you can. You should have a chance to say . . ." But I couldn't bring myself to utter the word good-bye.

We both climbed out and waded through the snow to the door. Max was bustling around inside, lifting boxes into a pile that he had begun to stack beside the door.

"What are you doing?" I asked, stepping inside the warm room and stomping the snow off my boots. It didn't hit me until after the question was out of my mouth that I should have greeted him with a hello. Maybe, "Merry Christmas." Anything other than the thoughtless query I blurted out. But he appeared so busy, so intent on whatever it was he was doing.

Max didn't seem to mind my rudeness. "Rachel." A smile creased his face as he settled the box he had been holding and crossed the room to give me a hug. He turned to Lily and held out his arms. She ran into them.

"Sarah told you?" I asked.

Max had ignored my first question, but he nodded in response to my second. "She told me enough. It's time for you to go."

"I'm scared," I admitted, casting a furtive glance at Lily. I didn't want her to know just how uncertain I was about the path we found ourselves on, but I needed Max's counsel more than I needed to keep up appearances. "I don't know where to go. I was thinking of heading south . . ."

"That's exactly what I had in mind," Max said with a secret smile.

It was then that I realized Max's eyes were sparkling in spite of the tense situation. I glanced around, wondering what was different in his store. Why he looked so pleased with himself.

"Where are Elena's fabrics?" I asked slowly. I took a few steps farther into the room and spun in a circle. Everything was gone. The silks and satins, the long lengths of organza, and even all the wools and tweeds that Max had used for his expensive suits. The shop was entirely bare.

"They're ready for you," he said indicating the stacks of boxes. "The contents are listed on the outside of each, and the Juki 8300 is packed away in its original box. Thread and needles, scissors, et cetera, are all in a separate Rubbermaid."

My mouth opened and closed, making little sounds that I had no control over whatsoever. Finally, I got hold of myself. "That sewing machine is worth eight hundred dollars," I reminded him. "And all that fabric . . . There must have been thousands of dollars worth of fabric left in your store."

"It's all yours." Max looked so happy he could hardly contain himself. "I've been packing for weeks. Most of it we'll have to ship, of course, but you can take a few of the boxes now."

"But—"

Max held up his hands to stop me. "I'm not trying to tell you what to do, Rachel. If you don't want to sew for a living, you don't have to. You can sell the fabrics and the machine and invest in whatever you want. But if you want to take the name of Eden Custom Tailoring—and keep my clients—I bequeath the shop and all that comes with it to you. Good thing it's a portable profession. And, by the way, a profitable one."

"You're giving us Eden?" Lily squeaked.

"Lock, stock, and barrel." Max caught my eye and winked. "It's always been yours anyway. Merry Christmas, sweetheart."

"Max . . ." I faltered, my heart so full of all that was his gift that there was no room for words, for anything other than gratitude.

"Oh," he thrust a finger in the air. "I almost forgot." Max hurried out of the storeroom and I could hear him rummaging around in the workroom desk. Within a minute he found what he was looking for and rushed back to hand it to me with a flourish.

The envelope was nondescript and labeled with nothing more than my name, front and center. But it was thick, and as I slid a finger under the flap I had a premonition of what was inside.

"I can't accept this," I exhaled, all the air in my lungs whooshing out of me in one long breath. I tried to hand the envelope back to Max, but he thrust his hands in his pockets and laughed like a little boy.

"You don't have a choice," he said. "It's yours. All of it."

There was a stack of bills inside the envelope, and when I flicked my fingers over the neat, green edges I realized that they were in denominations varying from twenty to one hundred dollars. It wasn't a fortune, but it was enough for hotels and food, gas to wherever it was we were going.

"That's just a portion of it," Max said, nodding at the envelope. "The rest is deposited in a bank account in your name. The account number and information are all written on the inside flap of the envelope."

I looked and sure enough, there was a series of numbers neatly written below the name and address of a bank in Flagstaff, Arizona. But before I could wonder at the location of the bank, I saw the amount that had been deposited: nine thousand dollars.

"I don't get it," I whispered.

"It's the remaining balance of my suit account. The check came in last week. You deserve every penny of it, Rachel. You've earned it."

Although I thought my tears had run dry, I found myself clinging to Max as I sobbed. At some point he held out an arm for Lily, and she snuggled right in between us, completing a trio that vacillated between laughter and tears. Eventually, Max gave me a fortifying squeeze and stepped back.

"My sister lives in Flagstaff, you know." He nodded at the envelope and the unexpected address of the bank. "She's expecting you. You don't have to stay—in fact, you don't have to go at all if you don't want to. The money can be transferred easily enough. But if you'd like, Meredith lives on a ranch just outside the city. It's beautiful there. Warm. She'd love the company until you've got your feet underneath you."

I was past the point of trying to assign words to everything I was thinking and feeling, so I caught Lily by the hand and shrugged one shoulder as if to say, "What do you think?"

"I've never been to Arizona," she said seriously. "But Katie's grandma lives there and she told me once that it smells like oranges. Does it smell like oranges?"

"The whole state," Max assured her. "And Meredith has her own tree. A pair of them, actually. And a couple of lemon trees, too."

Lily seemed to consider the possibility for a moment. Then she squeezed her eyes shut and nodded quickly, accepting our adventure with a courage that I couldn't help but admire.

"Okay," I said, laughter bubbling up inside me. "I guess we're on our way to Arizona."

"Perfect." Max reached a hand toward Lily and rested his palm against her cheek. "You won't have to wait until summer to wear your dress."

"But we never even started it." Lily shook her head.

"I think you and your mom will have plenty of time to sew something beautiful. You'll have to send me pictures."

We loaded the backseat and the storage compartment of the SUV from the floor to the roof with Max's carefully packed boxes. Only minutes before I had felt like I was leaving everything I knew and loved behind, but Max's indescribable gift had turned what felt like an exile into a grand adventure. We were taking a life with us. A wonderful life filled with meaning and possibility. Filled with hope.

But none of that negated the fact that it was hard to go, and after countless hugs and well wishes, Max had to shoo me and Lily out of his shop. I climbed reluctantly into the SUV and rolled down my window so that Max could lean in and give me last-minute instructions and directions. I thought we were finally ready to pull away when Max dug around in his pocket and produced a scrap of paper.

"There's just one more thing," he said, handing it to me.

And though I couldn't imagine that there was more, as I unfolded the little square of paper I knew that he had saved the best gift for last.

"I never wanted to take the place of your father, Rachel." Max gave my arm one last squeeze. "In fact, I always hoped that God would use me to lead you back to him.

I blinked at the address of a facility in a town less than an hour's drive from Everton. The Heritage Home.

"After all this time . . ." I breathed.

My daddy was just down the road.

It was a pretty establishment. Crisp white with neat, black trim and a sweeping front porch that gave it the look of a plantation. I drove through the roundabout and parked in one of the empty spaces as close to the entrance as I could get. The snow seemed to be getting deeper by the minute, and I was starting to worry that we would get snowed in. This would have to be a short visit. Short and sweet. And yet, even as I resigned myself to a quick good-bye, a part of me trembled at the thought of being close enough to touch him. I wasn't sure I'd be able to let go.

"I don't know what to expect," I said, turning the SUV off and twisting in my seat to regard Lily. "I haven't seen my father in over a decade. He could be sick or confused. He . . ." I trailed off, trying to imagine my father as the aged, decrepit man that I had just described. The image wouldn't come into focus. I lifted a shoulder as if I could shrug off the sad likeness. "Maybe you should wait by the front desk."

Lily's eyes sparked at the suggestion. "Are you kidding me? This is what I wanted, remember? I'm going to meet my grandfather."

"I don't understand why you're so excited to meet

him," I said, shaking my head. "It's not like you grew up with wonderful stories of him or anything."

The look on Lily's face pulled me up short. She seemed genuinely confused. "All of your stories of him are wonderful, Mom. Don't you see? He tried so hard. When he sewed your dress, when he bought you those cookies, when he played with you in the snow . . ." She laughed a little. "He didn't necessarily get it right, but he must have cared about you a lot to try."

I didn't know what to say. I had never really considered the fact that my dad did provide for me. He tried to be a dad—to show me that he loved me. There was the time he bought a book on hair braiding and attempted to learn how to French braid my hair. He was all thumbs and ended up creating a tangled mess that required half a bottle of detangler to undo. And the time I asked him to pick up a tube of eyeliner for me. He came back from the pharmacy with five different packages—each one a different brand and hue because he wanted to get it just right. Once Dad brought me a kitten because he thought I would like the company, and when the sweet fuzzball ran away he spent hours wandering around outside with a flashlight whispering, "Here kitty, kitty," into the dark. All at once a host of memories crowded and clamored for attention, and I put my hands to my head to press them back.

I had told Lily all about the quiet nights and the missed conversations, but the flip side of that particular coin was that my father worked very hard to give me a good life. When his body was weary and his spirit broken, he picked himself up every single day and gave himself over to a job that offered little more than a humble wage and the guarantee that he would be old before his time. I often thought my childhood was hard, but the truth was, I had wanted for nothing. My dad made sure of that.

Had I misunderstood everything? Or was Lily's youth and optimism painting my past with broad, rosy strokes? I wanted to ask my daughter more, to pick apart the grain of truth that she had offered up, but we simply didn't have time. The snow was accumulating on the windshield in swaths of winter white. "I'll make you a deal," I said. "Let me go in first. I need a little time alone with him before I introduce you."

"Fine." Lily nodded once. She stuck out her hand and we shook to seal the deal.

It was only seven o' clock in the evening, but The Heritage Home was enjoying a very silent night. A sacred hush seemed to have fallen over the place, almost as if the residents were all small children who were holding their breath in anticipation of Christmas morning. Our footsteps echoed on the tile floor of the entryway, disrupting the unearthly calm.

"Merry Christmas! Welcome to The Heritage Home." A perky young woman stood from her perch behind a large reception desk as we approached. "You don't look familiar to me—are you here to visit one of our guests?"

"Mitch—" I had to stop and clear my throat. "Mitchell Clark." His name felt peculiar on my tongue, foreign and familiar all at once, and I had to repress the urge to run. Did I want to run away? Or did I want to run down the hallways, calling for him until my father stepped from one of the rooms? I couldn't tell.

But before I could explore the snarl of my conflicting emotions, I realized that something in the woman's countenance had shifted at the sound of his name. She smiled at me a little sadly and said, "I should have seen it. You look just like him, you know."

"No, I don't." I didn't mean to be defensive, and I hurried to explain. "Everyone used to tell me I looked like my mother."

She lifted a hand in apology. "Well, you definitely have your father's eyes."

I didn't respond. I didn't know how to.

"Anyway," she knitted her fingers together and took a deep breath. "We've been waiting for you."

"What?" The word fell off my tongue and I reached for Lily's hand. Held it tight. "What do you mean?"

The woman flapped her hands weakly. "I'm sorry. I'm

making you uncomfortable, aren't I? Don't let me scare
you away! It's just . . . Oh, I don't know how to explain.
Let me call him." She tucked her bottom lip between her
teeth and grabbed the handset of a telephone, tapping in a
few numbers.

"My dad?" I asked. "Are you calling him?"

She shook her head and gave me and Lily her back.

I glanced at my daughter, more than a little unnerved
by our bizarre reception, but Lily wasn't watching the
drama unfold. As I followed her gaze, I realized her attention was completely absorbed by a massive Christmas tree
that stood in the lobby. It towered over us, and if the scent
in the air could be believed, it was real.

"May I?" Lily asked, looking up at me with wonder in
her eyes.

I smiled faintly and let her go, thankful that for the moment at least she was distracted from the strange scene that
was taking place behind the reception desk. The woman
was gesturing wildly, nodding her head, and talking excit-
edly into the phone. After a couple of minutes she hung
up and spun to give me a crooked grin.

"He'll be here in a jiffy."

"He?"

But instead of answering, she pretended not to hear me
and began to stack and restack papers that she tipped out
of a plastic filing box.

I heaved a sigh and joined Lily at the tree, making a show of studying the hodgepodge of mismatched ornaments so that I wouldn't seem so nervous. The truth was, my heart was struggling in my chest, flopping around like a fish out of water. I felt wholly out of my element, panicky and downright terrified of what awaited me in the depths of this alien land.

I wasn't accustomed to nursing homes. My nose wrinkled against the scent of disinfectant and age, the way that the stringent hospital air mingled with the fragrance of the Christmas tree. And the silence made me antsy—it was an awkward stillness, punctuated by eerie sounds I couldn't place but that I was sure heralded a life about to end without fanfare. Maybe even my father's life.

Was he confined to a wheelchair? Hooked up to machines? Would he curse at me for never once coming to see him even though I knew he was hurting? There were too many questions and I wasn't sure that I wanted to know the answers. Suddenly, I was overcome by an urge to leave. To grab Lily by the hand and bolt for the door before I made an even bigger mess of a messed-up life.

But it was too late for that now. My skin prickled as someone laid a hand on my shoulder.

"Rachel?"

I stiffened. That wasn't my dad's voice ... "Uncle Cooper?" I whispered, turning around.

"Hi, sweetheart."

Two words and I was undone. Before I even knew what I was doing, I was in his arms, hanging on for dear life. How many years had it been since I had seen Cooper? Surely, I was a little girl the last time we met. He was so much older than I remembered him, wrinkled and white, but his back was straight and I knew by the way he smiled at me that his mind was perfectly sound. My dad's older brother was still a man of great integrity and poise.

"Uncle Cooper, what are you doing here?" I asked, backing away so I could drink him in with my eyes. "I thought you were living in New York."

He tipped his head as if to tell me New York was a lifetime ago. "After I retired from the firm I found that the city didn't much suit me anymore. Then your dad had his stroke, and it just made sense that these two bachelor brothers should spend their final years together."

I narrowed my eyes, looking for any physical sign that my uncle needed to be in a care facility. He was eight years older than my dad, but as far as I could tell, Cooper looked fit and healthy for his age. "Why here?" I asked, hoping I wasn't being too forward in spite of all the years between us.

"We're just down the road from the best cancer hospital in the Midwest."

"Cancer?"

"Leukemia. They gave me six months to live."

"Oh, Cooper . . ."

"Honey, that was four years ago." Cooper winked.

"Why didn't you call me? I would have loved to know that you had left New York . . . that you were battling cancer . . ." I faltered, knowing that the wall between us was one that I had built. And yet . . .

"When I moved back, your dad made it very clear that you wanted your space. He said, 'If we love her, we have to respect her wishes. We have to let her go.' It might have been faulty logic—and believe me, it nearly killed your father to abide by his own edict—but he believed that one day you'd come around. And, well," he shrugged almost sheepishly, "you're here now."

It was exactly what Max had said: You're here now. One season of my life had rolled into the next and I finally found myself back where I began. Back where I belonged.

I put a hand to my forehead and tried to make sense of all the information that was coming at me. "I'm sorry," I said. "I'm a little overwhelmed right now."

"Me, too." Cooper smiled and looked past me, his expression softening as he regarded the child behind me.

Throwing up my arms, I blew a breath through my lips. "Oh, Uncle Cooper. What am I thinking? This is my daughter, Lily."

Lily was half hidden behind me, but when I introduced

her to Cooper she shot him a disarming smirk. "I didn't know I had an uncle," she said.

"Great-uncle." Cooper threw back his shoulders as if to emphasize that he fit the description. "It's very nice to meet you, Miss Lily."

"Very nice to meet you," she said, offering him her hand. Instead of shaking it, he lifted it to his lips. Lily's cheeks shone pink, but it was a delighted blush.

I glanced between them in a bit of a daze. In a very short time my world had tilted on its axis, and I would have loved nothing more than to cuddle down in one of the plush couches and talk with Uncle Cooper for hours. Even though I hadn't seen him much as a kid, my legendary big city uncle was a bright spot in my life. He was a wonderful listener, full of wisdom, and I could really use his sage counsel. But seeing him stirred up something else in me: an understanding that I had to see my dad. Now.

"He's here," Cooper said as if he could read my mind. "He's been waiting for you."

"What?"

Cooper shook his head. "You'll see. It's too hard to explain. But I think this will help."

I hadn't realized that Cooper was carrying anything until he handed me a fat manila envelope with a sense of ceremony. It was labeled with my name and the address of Cyrus's house in Everton, but I couldn't tell what was inside. Another envelope? I thought. My night seemed full of hidden magic.

"It's letters," Cooper explained so I didn't have to undo the clasp. "Dozens of them. Your dad started writing them shortly after the stroke, and he hasn't stopped for years. The first ones he was able to write, but as things got worse he dictated and I wrote. There's a notebook that I think he means for you to have, but these are the letters that I've written for him. I put each one in a separate envelope and dated it so you have some sort of pattern to follow, but I'm sure they're very repetitive. He's been pretty confused of late."

"Dad's been writing me letters?" I clutched the oversized envelope to my chest, uncertain how to respond. "Why didn't you send them?"

"I didn't know if you would read them. I wanted to wait until you were ready. Are you ready, Rachel?"

I chewed the inside of my cheek for a second, then gave him an earnest nod.

"He's sick, Rachel," Cooper began to explain. "It started pretty much right after the stroke. He doesn't remember everything—"

"I'm ready," I interrupted. I didn't know if I could handle all the nuts and bolts, the long list of ailments that I was suddenly sure afflicted the father I remembered as strong and whole. The last time I saw my dad we were barely on speaking terms, but he was healthy. And now, poised on the brink of finally seeing him again, I wasn't sure that I could reconcile the man in my mind with the person Cooper was trying to prepare me to meet. It was too much. There was only one thing that mattered: "I want to see my dad."

"Of course, honey. He wants to see you, too."

CHAPTER 18

MITCH

Christmas Eve, 7:30 P.M.

Mitch is startled by a knock at the door, and his heart stumbles over a bubble of sudden anticipation. He's waiting for something, for some-one, and though his mind can't remember, his heart does. Mitch turns from the window and smooths a hand over his tuft of downy hair, hoping. But the woman who peeks inside his room is unfamiliar. He can't help but deflate.

She's lovely, to be sure. Hair the color of burnt chestnuts and eyes that gleam like troubled water even from all the way across the room. But there is a weight on her shoulders that makes her bend beneath an unwieldy burden, and the expression on her face is indecipherable. Hesitation? Fear? Hope? Mitch isn't accustomed to such complexity in his nurses. Nor is he used to seeing the aides out of uniform. The tailored wool coat the woman is wearing is hardly standard issue.

"May I come in?" she asks. The request is so quiet it is almost a whisper. Mitch fights a wave of irritation.

"I'm waiting for someone," he tells her.

She straightens up a little and closes the door behind her with a soft click. "You are?"

Mitch merely nods, and returns his attention to the window where the snow still falls in lazy clumps. The dim room has turned the glass into a mirror, and in the gray reflection he can see the woman behind him pick at the buttons on her coat. She seems upset, but Mitch doesn't know how he can do anything about that. Besides, can't she see he's busy?

"I just wanted to say hello," she murmurs. Her long hair falls in curtains on either side of her face and for a moment Mitch can almost imagine what it would be like to reach over and tuck it behind her ears. It feels like an old reflex, bittersweet and somehow dear, but surely he would never dare to touch a stranger.

And then it hits him: She's not a stranger.

Mitch sucks in a quick breath as he tries to place the

pretty woman. Is she an old friend? A candy striper who retired her pink and white uniform? A niece, perhaps? But no, his brother lives in New York. He never married. Never had children.

Whether or not Mitch remembers her, the woman that hovers at the farthest edge of his small room is someone he should know. So, he stifles a grumpy sigh and mutters the only thing he can think of to say, "Hello."

She looks up and studies his face. Doesn't appear to find what she's looking for as her mouth twitches in a little frown. "It's me. Don't you remember me?" Before Mitch can formulate an answer, she shakes her head. "He told me that you didn't remember everything, but still. How could you forget...?"

The sorrow in her face is almost overwhelming, but Mitch can see that there is anger, too. She's mad at him, and something about that makes him mad, too. He doesn't have time for such games.

"I can't believe that you don't know who I am. After all this time. After everything we've been through ..." She rubs her forehead in frustration and squeezes her eyes shut as if she is battling a killer headache. "Fine," she huffs after a few tense seconds. "Whatever. I give up."

Mitch wonders if he should say something, but she doesn't give him a chance. "I guess it doesn't matter anyway now, because we're leaving." She says this as if it should mean something to him. But Mitch doesn't know who "we" are or where it is they think they're going. Is he supposed to care? He grunts noncommittally and she continues. "Not like you care, but we've been stuck in a pretty bad situation, and I think we're finally free."

"Good for you." Though he still resents the intrusion, Mitch is surprised to find that he is genuinely happy for her. There's nothing worse than a sweet girl in a bad situation. The woman with the sea-blue eyes seems sweet, even if she has an obvious chip on her shoulder.

"I guess I just wanted to say hello, and good-bye, before we leave. It's just ..." She closes her eyes and the lines of her face betray the long, hard road it's been. She sighs. "It's just been a very long time."

Mitch nods absently. A part of him wishes that he could place her and have a real conversation. She's obviously hurting. Looking for something that he can't give her. But a bigger part of him wishes that she would just go away. It's Christmas Eve, and the sense of longing that grips his chest is so overwhelming he can hardly think of anything else.

"I wanted you to know that I understand," she says, taking a few steps into the room. If she reached out, and if Mitch reached out for her, they could just touch fingertips. He doesn't mind her proximity. He can see the fine muscles in her neck work as she swallows and goes on. "I understand what it's like to love someone who probably doesn't merit that love. A long, long time ago you told me that everyone deserves . . ." she trails off. "But you don't remember that, do you? Just like you don't remember me."

It would probably be polite to assure her that he does, in fact, remember, but it would be a lie, and Mitch feels incapable of such pretense right now. Not tonight. Not on Christmas Eve, when he's clinging to a wish so distant he can hardly make out the contours of it from where he stands. He shakes his head.

"I didn't think you would." She looks sad. Absently, she raises her fingertips to her mouth and allows them to trace the curve of her bottom lip. It's an unconscious movement, a mannerism born of habit. All at once Mitch knows that she was a nail biter. When she was younger? In another life? Does it really matter? The hazy recollection is gone as quickly as it came, and in its place is the nagging impatience he feels at her unwanted company. This woman is interrupting his vigil.

"For whatever it's worth," she says, "I came here to tell you that I forgive you."

"You forgive me?" This is unexpected. Mitch tilts his head as he regards her, wondering what in the world he did to warrant a late-night, Christmas Eve absolution. He's about to tell the unfamiliar woman that she must have the wrong guy, surely she's mixed him up with someone else, when the sound of footsteps in the hall pulls him up short. There is the sound of a child's laughter, and then a rainstorm of light knocks on the door. His door. Mitch is so startled he can't speak.

He doesn't have to. The door eases open a crack and a white-haired man pokes his head through. "Mitch?" he says. "Can we come in for a moment?"

We? Mitch nods, barely able to control the motion of his own head. In turns it feels heavy as a stone and light as one of the snowflakes that drift outside his window. All Mitch can think is: I heard laugher. A little girl's laughter.

And then, before he can toss up one last wordless prayer, the door opens all the way and she is there. A cry escapes his lips.

She hasn't changed a bit. Cherry-pop hair in loose braids, errant curls framing her narrow face. A smattering of freckles dust her nose, and her blue eyes dance with a delight that she doesn't try to conceal or control. She's happy. Beautiful and happy, a vision so perfect she must surely be a dream.

But when she sees him, something in her faces changes. She freezes for a moment, and her smile flickers and then fades altogether. Mitch feels as if the room has darkened when she turns her eyes to the floor. Does she hate him? Is she angry for all the times he should have defended her but didn't? He wants to run to her and take her in his arms, but before he can do anything, the little girl peeks up at him from between dark lashes, and he realizes that she doesn't look upset: She looks suddenly shy. Like she wants desperately to reach out to him, but she doesn't quite dare.

Shy? Why would his own daughter be timid around him? Mitch opens his mouth to say her name, but at that moment the woman steps between them and puts her hands on the girl's thin shoulders.

"Now is not the time, honey."

Honey? Why is this strange woman calling his daughter honey?

"But I want to—"

"I said not now."

"But . . ." The child bites her lip and sneaks a glance at Mitch. Her eyes are full of things unsaid, and all at once Mitch knows that he is not the only one who has been waiting for this moment. It's almost more than he can bear. He's ready to throw the strange woman out of his room, but then the little girl nods obediently and tears her gaze from him.

"May I go outside while I wait?" she asks quietly. "Cooper says that it doesn't snow in Arizona, and this might be my last chance to play in the snow."

Mitch doesn't know who Cooper is or why his little girl cares about whether it snows in Arizona, but it doesn't matter. He takes a few tentative steps toward her, and when she doesn't back away, he dares to take a few more.

"You could make a snow angel," Mitch whispers tentatively. He clears his throat, tries again. "Do you know how to do that?"

Her smile is feather soft. "My mom taught me how to make them," she says. "She learned from her dad. I could show you if you'd like."

Mitch manages to croak, "I'd like that very much."

They've spoken; she isn't a dream. And yet all Mitch can do is gape. They stand there for what feels like forever, just looking at each other across a distance so small he can hear the faint exhalation of her warm breath. Mitch swallows her in hungry gulps, and she eyes him curiously. Almost as if she's seeing him for the very first time. Finally, she flashes him a brilliant smile and skips across the space between them to throw her arms around his waist. When she turns her face up, Mitch cups her cheeks, ignoring his own tears. Real men do cry, he decides. And real men tell their daughters how they feel.

He opens his mouth to do just that, to say the words he's kept inside for so long, but before he can, the woman speaks.

"Go outside and play," she commands the little girl. "We need some time alone."

The child sighs a little, but she slips out of Mitch's arms

and scurries to the door. "Stay right here, okay? I'll be back in a minute," she assures him, pausing for a moment with one hand on either side of the doorframe. "Watch me from the window!"

And just like that she's gone.

"I'll go with her." The tall man smiles, exchanging a private look with the woman who is still standing in Mitch's room.

Mitch is furious that she sent the child away, but he clings to the words that still linger in the room like a promise: I'll be right back. There is so much he wants to say to her! "Excuse me," he says, pushing past the woman so he can return to the window. He longs to press his hands against the glass—he doesn't want to miss a single second.

Instead of leaving, the woman walks quietly across the room and comes to stand beside him. She glances at him, and then touches her fingers to the cold pane of glass, her hand next to his in a parody of togetherness. Mitch doesn't mean to be rude, but his heart is bursting with the long-awaited realization of his hope, the wish so dear it nearly crushed his heart to dream it. He turns to the woman in exasperation.

"Look," Mitch says, "I don't know who you are, but I've been waiting ... for so long ..." his voice splinters and he can't go on.

"I can't believe you don't remember me. After everything . . ." The woman is crying now, too, and when she faces him he is struck by a sense of familiarity. Something inside him resonates with the slant of her eyes, the high curve of her cheekbone. But the echo is indistinct, and quieted completely when she says, "How could you not remember who I am?"

"I'm sorry." Mitch makes himself apologize, even though he's not sorry one bit. Can't she see that the only thing that matters right now is his little girl? "But I've been waiting so long for this day. I've prayed that she would come, that my daughter would come and see me one last time. And now she's here."

The room goes utterly still. "What?" the woman whispers. "What did you say? That was your daughter? The little girl with the braids?"

"Isn't she beautiful?"

The woman releases a long, shuddering breath. "Yes," she says. "She's beautiful."

"I've missed her so much."

"You have?"

"She's with me every minute of every day." Mitch doesn't know why he is telling all of this to a woman he doesn't know, but he can't seem to stop himself. "I want so badly to tell her . . ."

"Tell her what?"

"That I'm sorry. I've made so many mistakes," Mitch says. "I haven't always been there for her in the way that she needs me to be. I work so hard, and sometimes I forget that little girls just need someone to listen. I don't mean to fall asleep when she's talking."

"You don't?"

"Of course not. And I don't mean to mess everything up. I wanted her to wear that dress because it made her look so beautiful. You should see her in blue . . ."

"But—"

"And I should have defended her when her mother said those things, but Bev was hurting, too. All the pain of her childhood came out on our daughter. It was so wrong, but I didn't know how to stop it."

"You should have tried," the woman says quietly.

"I know." Mitch's voice breaks. "I should have tried."

They are silent for a moment, and in the stillness Mitch can feel all the things he wants to say fill his mouth. He's choking on memories, but though they are bitter, they are also sweet. "I wish that I knew how to connect with her," he says, "but I always seem to get it wrong. She's always one step ahead of me, and I'm trailing behind, wondering how I can help her understand that I'm here. And I always will be."

The woman covers her face with her hands, but a movement at the corner of his vision distracts Mitch. As he squints into the snowy landscape the child appears. She's struggling through the deep snow, her face radiant with laughter. Lifting her mittened hands to the sky, she catches a dozen snowflakes, then laps them up like a puppy. She is a pleasure to behold, a little girl on the very brink of her life, the innocence of her youth and the promise of her future woven together in a crown that seems to alight on her curls in the place where the streetlamp casts a pale luster. Mitch could watch her forever, but after a few minutes of kicking up the new-fallen snow, she seems to realize that she's being watched.

The girl straightens up and turns her attention to the bank of windows. She covers her brow with a mittened hand and squints as if she's looking for something.

"For me," Mitch murmurs with a rush of understanding. "She's looking for me."

"She's been looking for you for a very long time," the woman says. "Let her know you're watching. Wave at her."

Mitch does, waggling his fingers until the girl catches sight of him and waves back. Her excitement is a tangible thing, it tingles beneath his skin and fills all the empty places.

"I've waited so long to tell her . . ." Mitch trails off, lost in his own reverie.

"To tell her what? That you're sorry?"

"That I love her."

The woman inches her hand along the glass until Mitch can feel the warmth of her skin. He's surprised when she takes a deep breath and then covers his wrinkled knuckles with her own soft palm, soothing the arthritic knots of bone and flesh that haven't been held in more years than he can remember. It's a beautiful gesture, a moment of such unexpected sweetness Mitch makes a little sound in the back of his throat. He's been so lonely.

"She loves you, too," the woman says, squeezing.

Mitch can't help it, he catches her fingers in his own, interlocking them because it feels so good to hang on to someone. To be anchored to the world by the precious weight of another person. "How do you know?" he asks.

When she laughs, the sound is soft and light as air. She catches his eye in the reflection of the windowpane, and in the background he can still see the little girl making angels in the snow. "She loves you. She told me so."